THE LONGEST VOYAGE

Rovic addressed the Emperor. "As I told your man Guzan," he said, "what drew us hither was the tale that you were blessed with a Ship from heaven. And Guzan showed me this was true."

A hissing went down the hall. The princes grew stiff; even the guardsmen stirred and muttered. When the Emperor spoke, his voice had gone whetted: "Have you forgotten that these things are not for the uninitiate to see, Guzan?"

"No, Holy One," said the duke. Sweat sprang forth on his face. "However, his people also . . . his people are initiate too. Look at the marvels they brought. The tubes they have which make distant things look close at hand, such as he has given you, Holy One, is this not akin to the far-seer the Messenger possesses?"

"Poul Anderson is the creator of some of the most superb and memorable characters in science fiction!"
—*Frank Herbert*

SLOW LIGHTNING

I shuddered. "Would he really have eaten me?"

Gray nodded. "A Centaur has odd and rigid rules concerning what is a person and what is not: communication defines a person in most circumstances."

"Jesus! I could have talked to him!"

"If you *had* spoken, he might have challenged you to an eating duel."

"I can eat with the best of them!"

"An eating duel," said Gray carefully, "is a duel in which the loser gets eaten. To the Centaurs, losers are not persons by definition."

"Oh," I said, feeling very small.

"Steven Popkes is an audacious new talent and a welcome ad
—*Michael Swanwick*

D1628504

Also by Poul Anderson
Published by Tor Books

*Alight in the Void**
The Boat of a Million Years
Hoka! (with Gordon R. Dickson)
A Midsummer Tempest
No Truce with Kings
The Saturn Game
Tales of the Flying Mountains

THE PSYCHOTECHNIC LEAGUE:

The Psychotechnic League
Cold Victory
Starship

THE TIME PATROL:

The Shield of Time
*Tales of the Time Patrol**

* forthcoming

Poul ANDERSON
THE LONGEST VOYAGE

Steven POPKES
SLOW LIGHTNING

TOR

A TOM DOHERTY ASSOCIATES BOOK
NEW YORK

RIBBLE VALLEY

CLITHEROE

WHALLEY

051179319

This is a work of fiction. All the characters and events portrayed in
this book are fictitious, and any resemblance to real people or events
is purely coincidental.

THE LONGEST VOYAGE

Copyright © 1960 by Street & Smith Publications, Inc.

SLOW LIGHTNING

Copyright © 1991 by Steven Popkes

All rights reserved, including the right to reproduce this book, or
portions thereof, in any form.

A Tor Book
Published by Tom Doherty Associates, Inc.
49 West 24th Street
New York, N.Y. 10010

Cover art by Wayne Barlowe

ISBN: 0-812-51170-0

First Tor edition: February 1991

Printed in the United States of America

0 9 8 7 6 5 4 3 2 1

Poul ANDERSON
THE LONGEST VOYAGE

When first we heard of the Sky Ship, we were on an island whose name, as nearly as Montalirian tongues can wrap themselves about so barbarous a noise, was Yarzik. That was almost a year after the *Golden Leaper* sailed from Lavre Town, and we judged we had come halfway round the world. So befouled was our poor caravel with weeds and shells that all sail could scarce drag across the sea. What drinking water remained in the butts was turned green and evil, the biscuit was full of worms, and the first signs of scurvy had appeared on certain crewmen.

"Hazard or no," decreed Captain Rovic, "we must land somewhere." A gleam I remembered appeared in his eyes. He stroked his red beard

3

and murmured, "Besides, it's long since we asked for the Aureate Cities. Perhaps this time they'll have intelligence of such a place."

Steering by that ogre planet which climbed daily higher as we bore westward, we crossed such an emptiness that mutinous talk broke out afresh. In my heart I could not blame the crew. Imagine, my lords. Day upon day where we saw naught but blue waters, white foam, high clouds in a tropic sky; heard only the wind, *whoosh* of waves, creak of timbers, sometimes at night the huge sucking and rushing as a sea monster breached. These were terrible enough to common sailors, unlettered men who still thought the world must be flat. But then to have Tambur hang forever above the bowsprit, and climb, so that all could see we must eventually pass directly beneath that brooding thing . . . and what up-bore it? the crew mumbled in the forecastle. Would an angered God not let fall down on us?

So a deputation waited on Captain Rovic. Very timid and respectful they were, those rough burly men, as they asked him to turn about. But their comrades massed below, muscled sun-blackened bodies taut in the ragged kilts, with daggers and belaying pins ready to hand. We officers on the quarterdeck had swords and pistols, true. But we numbered a mere six, including that frightened boy who was myself, and aged Froad the astrologue, whose robe and white beard were reverend to see but of small use in a fight.

Rovic stood mute for a long while after the spokesman had voiced this demand. The stillness grew, until the empty shriek of wind in our shrouds, the empty glitter of ocean out to the world's rim, became all there was. Most splendid our master looked, for he had donned scarlet hose and bell-tipped shoon when he knew the deputation was coming; as well as helmet and corselet polished to mirror brightness. The plumes blew around that blinding steel head and the diamonds on his fingers flashed against the rubies in his sword hilt. Yet when at last he spoke, it was not as a knight of the Queen's court, but in the broad Anday of his fisher boyhood.

"So 'tis back ye'd wend, lads? Wi' a fair wind an' a warm sun, liefer ye'd come about an' beat half round the globe? How ye're changed from yere fathers! Ken ye nay the legend, that once all things did as man commanded, an' 'twas an Andayman's lazy fault that now men must work? For see ye, 'twas nay too much that he told his ax to cut down a tree for him, an' told the faggots to walk home, but when he told 'em to carry him, then God was wroth an' took the power away. Though to be sure, as recompense, God gave all Andaymen sea-luck, dice-luck, an' love-luck. What more d'ye ask for, lads?"

Bewildered at this response, the spokesman wrung his hands, flushed, looked at the deck, and stammered that we'd all perish miserably . . . starve, or thirst, or drown, or be crushed under that horrible moon, or sail off the world's edge . . . the *Golden Leaper* had come farther than ship had sailed since the Fall of Man, and if we returned at once, our fame would live forever—

"But can ye eat fame, Etien?" asked Rovic, still mild and smiling. "We've had fights an' storms, aye, an' merry carouses too; but devil an Aureate City we've seen, though well ye ken they lie out here someplace, stuffed wi' treasure for the first bold man who'll come plunder 'em. What ails yere gutworks, lad? Is't nay an easy cruise? What would the foreigners say? How will yon arrogant cavaliers o' Sathayn, yon grubby chapmen o' Woodland, laugh—nay alone at us, but at all Montalir—did we turn back!"

Thus he jollied them. Only once did he touch his sword, half drawing it, as if absentmindedly, when he recalled how we had weathered the hurricane off Xingu. But they remembered the mutiny that followed then, and how that same sword had pierced three armed sailors who attacked him together. His dialect told them he would let bygones lie forgotten: if they would. His bawdy promises of sport among lascivious heathen tribes yet to be discovered, his recital of treasure legends, his appeal to their pride as seamen and Montalirians, soothed fear. And then in the end, when he saw them malleable, he dropped the provincial speech. He stood forth on the quarterdeck with burning casque and tossing plumes, and the flag of Montalir blew its sea-faded colors above him, and he said as the knights of the Queen say:

"Now you know I do not propose to turn back until the great globe has been rounded and we bring to Her Majesty that gift which is most peculiarly ours to give. The which is not gold or slaves, nor even that lore of far places that she and her most excellent Company of Merchant Adventurers desire. No, what we shall lift in our hands to give her, on that day when again we lie by the long docks of Lavre, shall be our achievement: that we did this thing which no men have dared in all the world erenow, and did it to her glory.''

A while longer he stood, through a silence full of the sea's noise. Then he said quietly, ''Dismissed,'' turned on his heel, and went back into his cabin.

So we continued for some days more, the men subdued but not uncheerful, the officers taking care to hide their doubts. I found myself busied, not so much with the clerical duties for which I was paid or the study of captaincy for which I was apprenticed—both these amounting to little by now—as with assisting Froad, the astrologue. In these balmy airs he could carry on his work even on shipboard. To him it scarce mattered whether we sank or swam; he had lived more than a common span of years already. But the knowledge of the heavens to be gained here, that was something else. At night, standing on the foredeck with quadrant, astrolabe, and telescope, drenched in the radiance from above, he resembled some frosty-bearded saint in the window of Provien Minster.

''See there, Zhean.'' His thin hand pointed

7

above seas that glowed and rippled with light, past the purple sky and the few stars still daring to show themselves, toward Tambur. Huge it was in full phase at midnight, sprawling over seven degrees of sky, a shield or barry of soft vert and azure, splotched with angry sable that could be seen to move across its face. The firefly moon we had named Siett twinkled near the hazy edge of the giant. Balant, espied rarely and low on the horizon in our part of the world, here stood high: a crescent, but with the dark part of the disk tinged by luminous Tambur.

"Observe," declared Froad, "there's no doubt left, one can *see* how it rotates on an axis, and how storms boil up in its air. Tambur is no longer the dimmest of frightened legends, nor a dreadful apparition seen to rise as we entered unknown waters; Tambur is real. A world like our own. Immensely bigger, certes, but still a spheroid in space: around which our own world moves, always turning the same hemisphere to her monarch. The conjectures of the ancients are triumphantly confirmed. Not merely that our world is round, *pouf*, that's obvious to anyone . . . but that we move about a greater center, which in turn has an annual path about the sun. But, then, how big is the sun?"

"Siett and Balant are inner satellites of Tambur," I rehearsed, struggling for comprehension. "Vieng, Tarou, and the other moons commonly seen at home, have paths outside our own world's. Aye. But what holds it all up?"

"That I don't know. Mayhap the crystal sphere

8

containing the stars exerts an inward pressure. The same pressure, maybe, that hurled mankind down onto the earth, at the time of the Fall from Heaven.''

That night was warm, but I shivered, as if those had been winter stars. "Then," I breathed, "there may also be men on . . . Siett, Balant, Vieng . . . even on Tambur?"

"Who knows? We'll need many lifetimes to find out. And what lifetimes they'll be! Thank the good God, Zhean, that you were born in this dawn of the coming age."

Froad returned to making measurements. A dull business, the other officers thought; but by now I had learned enough of the mathematic arts to understand that from these endless tabulations might come the true size of the earth, of Tambur, sun and moons and stars, the path they took through space and the direction of Paradise. So the common sailors, who muttered and made signs against evil as they passed our instruments, were closer to fact than Rovic's gentlemen: for indeed Froad practiced a most potent gramarye.

At length we saw weeds floating on the sea, birds, towering cloud masses, all the signs of land. Three days later we raised an island. It was an intense green under those calm skies. Surf, still more violent than in our hemisphere, flung against high cliffs, burst in a smother of foam, and roared back down again. We coasted carefully, the palomers aloft to seek an approach, the gunners standing by our cannon with lighted matches. For not only were there unknown currents and shoals—familiar hazards—but we had had brushes with canoe-sailing cannibals in the past. Especially did we fear the eclipses. My lords can visualize how in that hemisphere the sun each day must go behind Tambur. In that longitude the occurrence was about midafternoon and lasted nearly ten minutes. An awesome sight: the primary planet—for so Froad now called it, a planet akin to Diell or Coint, with our own world humbled to a mere satellite thereof!—become a black disk encircled with red, up in a sky suddenly full of stars. A cold wind blew across the sea, and even the breakers seemed hushed. Yet so impudent is the soul of man that we continued about our duties, stopping only for the briefest prayer as the sun disappeared, thinking more about the chance of shipwreck in the gloom than of God's Majesty.

So bright is Tambur that we continued to work our way around the island at night. From sunup to sunup, twelve mortal hours, we kept the *Golden Leaper* slowly moving. Toward the second noon, Captain Rovic's persistence was rewarded. An opening in the cliffs revealed a long fjord. Swamp shores overgrown with saltwater trees told us that while the tides rose high in that bay, it was not one of those roosts so dreaded by mariners. The wind being against us, we furled sail and lowered the boats, towing in our caravel by the power of oars. This was a vulnerable moment, especially since we had perceived a village within the fjord. "Should we not stand out,

master, and let them come first to us?'' I ventured.

Rovic spat over the rail. ''I've found it best
never to show doubt,'' said he. ''If a canoe fleet
should assail us, we'll give 'em a whiff of grape-
shot and trust to break their nerve. But I think,
thus showing ourselves fearless of them from the
very first, we're less likely to meet treacherous
ambuscade later.''

He proved right.

In the course of time, we learned we had come
upon the eastern end of a large archipelago. The
inhabitants were mighty seafarers, considering
that they had only outrigger dugouts to travel in.
These, however, were often a hundred feet long.
With forty paddles, or with three bast-sailed
masts, such a vessel could almost match our best
speed, and was more maneuverable. However,
the small cargo space limited their range of
travel.

Though they lived in houses of wood and
thatch, possessing only stone tools, the natives
were cultivated folk. They farmed as well as
fished; their priests had an alphabet. Tall and
vigorous, somewhat darker and less hairy than
we, they were impressive to behold: whether
nude as was common, or in full panoply of cloth
and feathers and shell ornaments. They had
formed a loose empire through the archipelago,
raided islands lying farther north, and carried on
a brisk trade within their own borders. Their
whole nation they called the Hisagazi, and the
island on which we had chanced was Yarzik.

This we learned slowly, as we mastered somewhat their tongue. For we were several weeks at that town. The duke of the island, Guzan, made us welcome, supplying us with food, shelter, and helpers as we required. For our part, we pleased them with glassware, bolts of Wondish cloth, and suchlike trade goods. Nonetheless we encountered many difficulties. The shore above high-water mark being too swampy for beaching a vessel as heavy as ours, we must build a drydock before we could careen. Numerous of us took a flux from some disease, though all recovered in time, and this slowed us further.

"Yet I think our troubles will prove a blessing," Rovic told me one night. As had become his habit, once he learned I was a discreet amanuensis, he confided certain thoughts in me. The captain is ever a lonely man; and Rovic, fisher lad, freebooter, self-taught navigator, victor over the Grand Fleet of Sathayn and ennobled by the Queen herself, must have found the keeping of that necessary aloofness harder than would a gentleman born.

I waited silent, there in the grass hut they had given him. A soapstone lamp threw wavering light and enormous shadows over us; something rustled the thatch. Outside, the damp ground sloped past houses on stilts and murmurous fronded trees, to the fjord where it shimmered under Tambur. Faintly I heard drums throb, a chant and stamping of feet around some sacrificial fire. Indeed the cool hills of Montalir seemed far.

Rovic leaned back in his muscular form, y-clad in a mere seaman's kilt in this heat. He had had them fetch him a civilized chair from the ship. "For see you, young fellow," he continued, "at other times we'd have established just enough communication to ask about gold. Well, we might also try to get a few sailing directions. But all in all, we'd hear little except the old story—'aye, foreign lord, indeed there's a kingdom where the very streets are paved with gold . . . a hundred miles west'—anything to get rid of us, eh? But in this prolonged stay, I've asked out the duke and the idolater priests more subtly. I've been so coy about whence we came and what we already know, they've let slip a gobbet of knowledge they'd not otherwise have disgorged on the rack itself."

"The Aureate Cities?" I cried.

"Hush! I'd not have the crew get excited and out of hand. Not yet."

His leathery, hook-nosed face turned strange with thought. "I've always believed those cities an old wives' tale," he said. My shock must have been mirrored to his gaze, for he grinned and went on, "A useful one. Like a lodestone on a stick, it's dragging us around the world." His mirth faded. Again he got that look, which was not unlike the look of Froad considering the heavens. "Aye, of course I want gold, too. But if we find none on this voyage, I'll not care. I'll just capture a few ships of Eralia or Sathayn when we're back in home waters, and pay for the voyage thus. I spoke God's truth that day on the

13

quarterdeck, Zhean, that this jorney was its own goal; until I can give it to Queen Odela, who once gave me the kiss of ennoblement.''

He shook himself out of his reverie and said in a brisk tone: ''Having led him to believe I already knew the most of it, I teased from Duke Guzan the admission that on the main island of this Hisagazi empire is something I scarce dare think about. A ship of the gods, he says, and an actual live god who came from the stars therein. Any of the natives will tell you this much. The secret reserved to the noble folk is that this is no legend or mummery, but sober fact. Or so Guzan claims. I know not what to think. But . . . he took me to a holy cave and showed me an object from that ship. It was some kind of clockwork mechanism, I believe. What, I know not. But of a shining silvery metal such as I've never seen before. The priest challenged me to break it. The metal was not heavy; must have been thin. But it blunted my sword, splintered a rock I pounded with, and my diamond ring would not scratch it.''

I made signs against evil. A chill went along me, spine and skin and scalp, until I prickled all over. For the drums were muttering in a jungle dark, and the waters lay like quicksilver beneath gibbous Tambur, and each afternoon that planet ate the sun. Oh, for the bells of Provien, across windswept Anday downs!

When the *Golden Leaper* was seaworthy again, Rovic had no trouble gaining permission to visit the Hisagazian emperor on the main island. He would, indeed, have found difficulty in not doing so. By now the canoes had borne word of us from one end of the realm to another, and the great lords were agog to see these blue-eyed strangers. Sleek and content once more, we disentangled ourselves from the arms of tawny wenches and embarked. Up anchor, up sail, with chanties whose echoes sent sea birds whirling above the steeps, and we stood out to sea. This time we were escorted. Guzan himself was our pilot, a big middle-aged man whose handsomeness was not much injured by the livid green tattoos his folk affected on face and body. Several of his sons spread their pallets on our decks, while a swarm of warriors paddled alongside.

Rovic summoned Etien the boatswain to him in his cabin. "You're a man of some wit," he said. "I give you charge of keeping our crew alert, weapons ready, however peaceful this may look."

"Why, master!" The scarred brown face sagged with near dismay. "Think you the natives plot a treachery?"

"Who can tell?" said Rovic. "Now, say naught to the crew. They've no skill in dissembling. Did greed or fear rise among 'em, the natives would sense as much, and grow uneasy—which would worsen the attitude of our own men, until none but God's Daughter could tell what'd happen. Only see to it, as casually as you're able, that our arms are ever close by and that our folk stay together."

15

Etien collected himself, bowed, and left the cabin. I made bold to ask what Rovic had in mind.

"Nothing, yet," said he. "However, I did hold in these fists a piece of clockwork such as the Grand Ban of Giair never imagined; and yarns were spun me of a Ship which flew down from heaven, bearing a god or a prophet. Guzan thinks I know more than I do, and hopes we'll be a new, disturbing element in the balance of things, by which he may further his own ambitions. He did not take all those fighting men along by accident. As for me . . . I intend to learn more about this."

He sat a while at his table, staring at a sunbeam which sickled up and down the wainscot as the ship rocked. Finally: "Scripture tells us man dwelt beyond the stars before the Fall. The astrologues of the past generation or two have told us the planets are corporeal bodies like this earth. A traveler from Paradise—"

I left with my head in a roar.

We made an easy passage among scores of islands. After several days we raised the main one, Ulas-Erkila. It is about a hundred miles long, forty miles across at the widest, rising steep and green toward central mountains dominated by a volcanic one. The Hisagazi worship two sorts of gods, watery and fiery, and believe this Mount Ulas houses the latter. When I saw that snow-peak afloat in the sky above emerald ridges, staining the blue with smoke, I could feel what the pagans did. The holiest act a man can perform among them is to cast himself into the burning crater of Ulas, and many an aged warrior is carried up the mountain that he may do so. Women are no allowed on the slopes.

Nikum, the royal seat, is situated at the head of a fjord like the village where we had been staying. But Nikum is rich and extensive, being about the size of Roann. Many houses are made from timber rather than thatch; there is also a massive basalt temple atop a cliff, overlooking the city, with orchards, jungle, and mountains at its back. So great are the tree trunks available to them for pilings, the Hisagazi have built here a regular set of docks like those at Lavre—instead of moorings and floats that can rise or fall with the tides, such as most harbors throughout the world are content with. We were offered a berth of honor at the central wharf, but Rovic made the excuse that our ship was awkward to handle and got us tied at the far end.

"In the middle, we'd have the watchtower straight above us," he muttered to me. "And they may not have discovered the bow here, but their javelin throwers are good. Also, we'd have an easy approach to our ship, plus a clutter of moored canoes between us and the bay mouth. Here, though, a few of us could hold the pier whilst the others ready for quick departure."

"But have we anything to fear, master?" I asked.

He gnawed his mustache. "I know not. Much depends on what they really believe about this god ship of theirs . . . as well as what the truth

17

is. But come all death and hell against us, we'll not return without that truth for Queen Odela.''

Drums rolled and feathered spearmen leaped as our officers disembarked. A royal catwalk had been erected above high-water level. (Common townsfolk in this realm swim from house to house when the tide laps their thresholds, or take a coracle if they have burdens to carry.) Across the graceful span of vines and canes lay the palace, which was a long building made from logs, the roof pillars carved into fantastic god shapes.

Iskilip, Priest-Emperor of the Hisagazi, was an old and corpulent man. A soaring headdress of plumes, a feather robe, a wooden scepter topped with a human skull, his own facial tattoos, his motionlessness, all made him seem unhuman. He sat on a dais, under sweet-smelling torches. His sons sat cross-legged at his feet, his courtiers on either side. Down the long walls were ranged his guardsmen. They had not our custom of standing to attention; but they were big supple young men, with shields and corselets of scaly sea-monster leather, with flint axes and obsidian spears that could kill as easily as iron. Their heads were shaven, which made them look the fiercer.

Iskilip greeted us well, called for refreshment, bade us be seated on a bench not much lower than his dais. He asked many perceptive questions. Wide-ranging, the Hisagazi knew of islands far beyond their own chain. They could even point the direction and tell us roughly the distance of a many-castled country they named

Yurakadak, though only one of them had traveled that far himself. Judging by their third-hand description, what could this be but Giair, which the Wondish adventurer Hanas Tolasson had reached overland? It blazed in me that we were indeed rounding the world. Only after that glory had faded a little did I again heed the talk.

"As I told Guzan," Rovic was saying, "another thing which drew us hither was the tale that you were blessed with a Ship from heaven. And he showed me this was true."

A hissing went down the hall. The princes grew stiff, the courtiers blanked their countenances, even the guardsmen stirred and muttered. Remotely through the walls I heard the rumbling, nearing tide. When Iskilip spoke, through the mask of himself, his voice had gone whetted: "Have you forgotten that these things are not for the uninitiate to see, Guzan?"

"No, Holy One," said the duke. Sweat sprang forth among the devils on his face, but it was not the sweat of fear. "However, this captain knew. His people also . . . as nearly as I could learn . . . he still has trouble speaking so I can understand . . . his people are initiate too. The claim seems reasonable, Holy One. Look at the marvels they brought. The hard, shining stone-which-is-not-stone, as in this long knife I was given, is that not like the stuff of which the Ship is built? The tubes which make distant things look close at hand, such as he has given you, Holy One, is this not akin to the far-seer the Messenger possesses?"

Iskilip leaned forward, toward Rovic. His scepter hand trembled so much that the pegged jaws of the skull clattered together. "Did the Star People themselves teach you to make all this?" he cried. "I never imagined . . . the Messenger never spoke of any others—"

Rovic held up both palms. "Not so fast, Holy One, I pray you," said he. "We are poorly versed in your tongue. I couldn't recognize a word just now."

This was his deceit. All his officers had been ordered to feign a knowledge of Hisagazi less than they really possessed. (We had improved our command of it by secret practicing with each other.) Thus he had an unimpeachable device for equivocation.

"Best we talk of this in private, Holy One," suggested Guzan, with a glare at the courtiers. They returned him a jealous glare.

Iskilip slouched in his gorgeous regalia. His words fell blunt enough, but in the weak tone of an old, uncertain man. "I know not. If these strangers are already initiate, certes we can show them what we have. But otherwise—if profane ears heard the Messenger's own tale—"

Guzan raised a dominator's hand. Bold and ambitious, long thwarted in his petty province, he had taken fire this day. "Holy One," he said, "why has the full story been withheld all these years? In part to keep the commoners obedient, aye. But also, did you and your councillors not fear that all the world might swarm hither, greedy

20

for knowledge, if it knew, and we should then be overwhelmed? Well, if we let the blue-eyed men go home with curiosity unsatisfied, I think they are sure to return in strength. So we have naught to lose by revealing the truth to them. If they have never had a Messenger of their own, if they can be of no real use to us, time enough to kill them. But if they have indeed been visited like us, what might we and they not do together!''

This was spoken fast and softly, so that we Montalirians should not understand. And indeed our gentlemen failed to do so. I, having young ears, got the gist; and Rovic preserved such a fatuous smile of incomprehension that I knew he was seizing every word.

So in the end they decided to take our leader— and my insignificant self, for no Hisagazian magnate goes anywhere quite unattended—up to the temple. Iskilip led the way in person, with Guzan and two brawny princes behind. A dozen spearmen brought up the rear. I thought Rovic's blade would be of scant use if trouble came, but set my lips firmly together and made myself walk behind him. He looked as eager as a child on Thanksday Morning, teeth agleam in the pointed beard, a plumed bonnet slanted rakish over his brow. None would have thought him aware of any peril.

We left about sundown; in Tambur's hemisphere, folk make less distinction between day and night than our people must. Having observed Siett and Balant in high tide position, I

was not surprised that Nikum lay nearly
drowned. And yet, as we wound up the cliff trail
toward the temple, methought I had never seen
a view more alien.

Below us lay a sheet of water, on which the
long grass roofs of the city appeared to float; the
crowded docks, where our own ship's masts and
spars raked above heathen figureheads; the fjord,
winding between precipices toward its mouth,
where the surf broke white and terrible on the
skerries. The heights above us seemed altogether
black, against a fire-colored sunset that filled
nigh half the sky and bloodied the waters. Wan
through those clouds I glimpsed the thick crescent of Tambur, banded in a heraldry no man
could read. A basalt column chipped into the
shape of a head loomed in outline athwart the
planet. Right and left of the path grew saw-
toothed grasses, summer dry. The sky was pale
at the zenith, dark purple in the east, where the
first few stars had appeared. Tonight I found no
comfort in the stars. We all walked silent. The
bare native feet made no noise. My own shoes
went *pad-pad* and the bells on Rovic's toes raised
a tiny jingle.

The temple was a bold piece of work. Within
a quadrangle of basalt walls guarded by tall stone
heads lay several buildings of the same material.
Only the fresh-cut fronds that roofed them were
alive. With Iskilip to lead us, we brushed past
acolytes and priests to a wooden cabin behind
the sanctum. Two guardsmen stood watch at its

door, but they knelt for Iskilip. The emperor rapped with his curious scepter.

My mouth was dry and my heart thunderous. I expected almost any being hideous or radiant to stand in the doorway as it was opened. Astonishing, then, to see just a man, and of no great stature. By lamplight within I discerned his room, clean, austere, but not uncomfortable; this could have been any Hisagazian dwelling. He himself wore a simple bast skirt. The legs beneath were bent and thin, old man's shanks. His body was also thin, but still erect, the white head proudly carried. In complexion he was darker than a Montalirian, lighter than a Hisagazian, with brown eyes and thin beard. His visage differed subtly, in nose and lips and slope of jaw, from any other race I had ever encountered. But he was human.

Naught else.

We entered the cabin, shutting out the spearmen. Iskilip doddered through a half-religious ceremony of introduction. I saw Guzan and the princes shift their stance, restless and unawed. Their class had long been party to this. Rovic's face was unreadable. He bowed with full courtliness to Val Nira, Messenger of Heaven, and explained our presence in a few words. But as he spoke, their eyes met and I saw him take the star man's measure.

"Aye, this is my home," said Val Nira. Habit spoke for him; he had given this account to so many young nobles that the edges were worn off it. As yet he had not observed our metallic in-

struments, or else had not grasped their signifi-
cance to him. "For . . . forty-three years, is that
right, Iskilip? I have been treated as well as might
be. If at times I was near screaming from lone-
liness, that is what an oracle must expect."

The emperor stirred, uneasy in his robe. "His
demon left him," he explained. "Now he is simple human flesh. That's the real secret we keep.
It was not ever thus. I remember when he first
came. He prophesied immense things, and all
the people wailed and went on their faces. But
sithence his demon has gone back to the stars,
and the once potent weapon he bore has equally
been emptied of its force. The people would not
believe this, however, so we still pretend otherwise, or there would be unrest among them."

"Affecting your own privileges," said Val
Nira. His tone was tired and sardonic. "Iskilip
was young then," he added to Rovic, "and the
imperial succession was in doubt. I gave him my
influence. He promised in return to do certain
things for me."

"I tried, Messenger," said the monarch. "Ask
all the sunken canoes and drowned men if I did
not try. But the will of the gods was otherwise."

"Evidently," Val Nira shrugged. "These islands have few ores, Captain Rovic, and no person capable of recognizing those I required. It's
too far to the mainland for Hisagazian canoes.
But I don't deny you tried, Iskilip . . . then."
He cocked an eyebrow back at us. "This is the
first time foreigners have been taken so deeply

into the imperial confidence, my friends. Are you certain you can get back out again, alive?''

"Why, why, why, they're our guests!'' blustered Iskilip and Guzan, almost in each other's mouths.

"Besides,'' smiled Rovic, "I had most of the secret already. My own country has secrets of its own, to set against this. Yes, I think we might well do business, Holy One.''

The emperor trembled. His voice cracked across. "Have you indeed a Messenger too?''

"What?'' For a numbed moment Val Nira stared at us. Red and white pursued each other across his countenance. Then he sat down on the bench and began to weep.

"Well, not precisely.'' Rovic laid a hand on the shaking shoulder, "I confess no heavenly vessel had docked at Montalir. But we've certain other secrets, belike equally valuable.'' Only I, who knew his moods somewhat, could sense the tautness in him. He locked eyes with Guzan and stared the duke down as a wild animal tamer does. And all the while, motherly gentle, he spoke with Val Nira. "I take it, friend, your Ship was wrecked on these shores, but could be repaired if you had certain materials?''

"Yes . . . yes . . . listen—'' Stammering and gulping at the thought he might see his home again ere he died, Val Nira tried to explain.

The doctrinal implications of what he said are so astounding, even dangerous, that I feel sure my lords would not wish me to repeat much. However, I do not believe they are false. If the

25

stars are indeed suns like our own, each attended by planets like our own, this demolishes the crystal-sphere theory. But Froad, when he was told later, did not think that mattered to the true religion. Scripture has never said in so many words that Paradise lies directly above the birth-place of God's Daughter; this was merely assumed, during those centuries when the earth was believed to be flat. Why should Paradise not be those planets of other suns, where men dwell in magnificence, men who possess all the ancient arts and flit from star to star as casually as we might go from Lavre to West Alayn?

Val Nira believed our ancestors had been cast away on this world, several thousand years ago. They must have been fleeing the consequences of some crime or heresy, to come so far from any human domain. Somehow their ship was wrecked, the survivors went back to savagery, only by degrees have their descendants regained a little knowledge. I cannot see where this explanation contradicts the dogma of the Fall. Rather, it amplifies it. The Fall was not the portion of all mankind, but only of a few—our own tainted blood—while the others continued to dwell prosperous and content in the heavens.

Even today, our world lies far off the trade lanes of the Paradise folk. Very few of them nowadays have any interest in seeking new worlds. Val Nira, though, was such a one. He traveled at hazard for months until he chanced upon our earth. Then the curse seized him, too.

Something went wrong. He descended upon Ulas-Erkila, and the Ship would fly no more.

"I know what the damage is," he said ardently. "I've not forgotten. How could I? No day has passed in all these years that I didn't recite to myself what must be done. A certain subtle engine in the Ship requires quicksilver." (He and Rovic must spend some time talking ere they deduced this must be what he meant by the word he used.) "When the engine failed, I landed so hard that its tanks burst. All the quicksilver, what I had in reserve as well as what I was employing, poured forth. So much, in that hot enclosed space, would have poisoned me. I fled outside, forgetting to close the doorway. The deck being canted, the quicksilver ran after me. By the time I had recovered from blind panic, a tropical rainstorm had carried off all the fluid metal. A series of unlikely accidents, yes, that's what's condemned me to a life's exile. It really would have made more sense to perish outright!"

He clutched Rovic's hand, staring up from his seat at the captain who stood over him. "Can you actually get quicksilver?" he begged. "I need no more than the volume of a man's head. Only that, and a few repairs easily made with tools in the Ship. When this cult grew up around me, I must needs release certain things I possessed, that each provincial temple might have a relic. But I took care never to give away anything important. Whatever I need is all there. A gallon of quicksilver, and—Oh, God, my wife may even be alive, on Terra!"

* * *

Guzan, at least, had begun to understand the situation. He gestured to the princes, who hefted their axes and stepped a little closer. The door was shut on the guard escort, but a shout would bring their spears into this cabin. Rovic looked from Val Nira to Guzan, whose face was grown ugly with tension. My captain laid hand on hilt. In no other way did he seem to feel any nearness of trouble.

"I take it, milord," he said lightly, "you're willing that the Heaven Ship be made to fly again."

Guzan was jarred. He had never expected this. "Why, of course," he exclaimed. "Why not?"

"Your tame god would depart you. What then becomes of your power in Hisagazi?"

"I . . . I'd not thought of that," Iskilip stuttered.

Val Nira's eyes shuttled among us, as if watching a game of paddleball. His thin body shook. "No," he whimpered. "You can't. You can't keep me!"

Guzan nodded. "In a few more years," he said, not unkindly, "you would depart in death's canoe anyhow. If meanwhile we held you against your will, you might not speak the right oracles for us. Nay, be at ease; we'll get your flowing stone." With a slitted glance at Rovic: "Who shall fetch it?"

"My own folk," said the knight. "Our ship can readily reach Giair, where there are civilized nations who surely have the quicksilver. We could return within a year, I think.''

''Accompanied by a fleet of adventurers, to help you seize the sacred vessel?'' asked Guzan bluntly. ''Or . . . once out of our islands . . . you might not proceed to Yurakadak at all. You might continue the whole way home, and tell your Queen, and return with all the power she commands.''

Rovic lounged against a roof post, like a big pouncecat at its ease in ruffles and hose and scarlet cape. His right hand continued to rest on his sword pommel. ''Only Val Nira could make that Ship go, I suppose,'' he drawled. ''Does it matter who aids him in making repairs? Surely you don't think either of our nations could conquer Paradise!''

''The Ship is very easy to operate,'' chattered Val Nira. ''Anyone can fly it in air. I showed many nobles what levers to use. It's navigating among the stars which is more difficult. No nation on this world could even reach my people unaided—let alone fight them—but why should you think of fighting? I've told you a thousand times, Iskilip, the dwellers in the Milky Way are dangerous to none, helpful to all. They have so much wealth they're hard put to find a use for most of it. Gladly would they spend large amounts to help all the peoples on this world become civilized again.'' With an anxious, half-hysterical look at Rovic: ''Fully civilized, I mean. We'll teach you our arts. We'll give you engines, automata, homunculi, that do all the toilsome work; and boats that fly through the air; and regular passenger service on those ships that ply between the stars—''

"These things you have promised for forty years," said Iskilip. "We've only your word."

"And, finally, a chance to confirm his word," I blurted.

Guzan said with calculated grimness: "Matters are not that simple, Holy One. I've watched these men from across the ocean for weeks, while they lived on Yarzik. Even on their best behavior, they're a fierce and greedy lot. I trust them no further than my eyes reach. This very night I see how they've befooled us. They know our language better than they ever admitted. And they misled us to believe they might have some inkling of a Messenger. If the Ship were indeed made to fly again, with them in possession, who knows what they might choose to do?''

Rovic's tone softened still further, "What do you propose, Guzan?"

"We can discuss that another time."

I saw knuckles tighten around stone axes. For a moment, only Val Nira's unsteady breathing was heard. Guzan stood heavy in the lamplight, rubbing his chin, the small black eyes turned downward in thoughtfulness. At last he shook himself. "Perhaps," he said crisply, "a crew mainly Hisagazian could sail your ship, Rovic, and fetch the flowing stone. A few of your men could go along to instruct ours. The rest could remain here as hostages."

My captain made no reply. Val Nira groaned,

"You don't understand! You're squabbling over nothing! When my people come here, there'll be no more war, no more oppression, they'll cure you of all such diseases. They'll show friendship to all and favor to none. I beg you—"

"Enough," said Iskilip. His own words fell ragged. "We shall sleep on all this. If anyone can sleep after so much strangeness."

Rovic looked past the emperor's plumes, into the face of Guzan. "Before we decide anything—" His fingers tightened on the sword hilt till the nails turned white. Some thought had sprung up with him. But he kept his tone even. "First I want to see that Ship. Can we go there tomorrow?"

Iskilip was the Holy One, but he stood huddled in his feather robe. Guzan nodded agreement.

We bade our good nights and went forth under Tambur. The planet was waxing toward full, flooding the courtyard with cold luminance, but the hut was shadowed by the temple. It remained a black outline, with a narrow lamplight rectangle of doorway in the middle. There was etched the frail body of Val Nira, who had come from the stars. He watched us till we had gone out of sight.

On the way down the path, Guzan and Rovic bargained in curt words. The Ship lay two days' march inland, on the slopes of Mount Ulas. We would go in a joint party to inspect it, but a mere

31

dozen Montalirians were to be allowed. Afterward we would debate our course of action.

Lanthorns glowed yellow at our caravel's poop. Refusing Iskilip's hospitality, Rovic and I returned thither for the night. A pikeman on guard at the gangway inquired what I had learned. "Ask me tomorrow," I said feebly. "My head's in too much of a whirl."

"Come into my cabin, lad, for a stoup ere we retire," the captain invited me.

God knows I needed wine. We entered the low little room, crowded with nautical instruments, with books, and with printed charts that looked quaint to me now I had seen a little of those spaces where the cartographer drew mermaids and windsprites. Rovic sat down behind his table, gestured me to a chair opposite, and poured from a carafe into two goblets of Quaynish crystal. Then I knew he had momentous thoughts in his head—far more than the problem of saving our lives.

We sipped a while, unspeaking. I heard the *lap-lap* of wavelets on our hull, the tramp of men on watch, the rustle of distant surf: otherwise nothing. At last Rovic leaned back, staring at the ruby wine on the table. I could not read his expression.

"Well, lad," said he, "what do you think?"

"I know not what to think, master."

"You and Froad are a little prepared for this idea that the stars are other suns. You're educated. As for me, I've seen so much eldritch in

my day that this seems quite believable. The rest
of our people, though—''

"An irony that barbarians like Guzan should
long have been familiar with the concept—
having had the old man from the sky to preach
it privily to their class for more than forty years—
Is he indeed a prophet, master?''

"He denies it. He plays prophet because he
must, but it's evident all the dukes and earls of
this realm know it's a trick. Iskilip is senile, more
than half converted to his own artificial creed.
He was mumbling about prophecies Val Nira
made long ago, true prophecies. Bah! Tricks of
memory and wishfulness. Val Nira is a human
and fallible as I am. We Montalirians are the
same flesh as these Hisagazi, even if we have
learned the use of metal before they did. Val
Nira's people know more in turn than us; but
they're still mortals, by Heaven. I *must* remember that they are.''

"Guzan remembers.''

"Bravo, lad!'' Rovic's mouth bent upward,
one-sidedly. "He's a clever one, and bold. When
he came, he saw his chance to stop stagnating as
the petty lord of an outlying island. He'll not let
that chance slip without a fight. Like many a
double-dealer before him, he accuses us of plotting the very things he hopes to do.''

"But what does he hope for?''

"My guess would be, he wants the Ship for
himself. Val Nira said it was easy to fly. Navigation between the stars would be too difficult
for anyone save him; nor could any man in his

right mind hope to play pirate along the Milky Way. However . . . if the Ship stayed right here, on this earth, rising no higher than a mile above ground . . . the warlord who used it might conquer more widely than Lame Darveth himself.''

I was aghast. ''Do you mean Guzan would not even try to seek out Paradise?''

Rovic scowled so blackly at his wine that I saw he wanted aloneness. I stole off to my bunk in the poop.

The captain was up before dawn, readying our folk. Plainly he had reached some decision, and it was not pleasant. But once he set a course, he seldom left it. He was long in conference with Etien, who came out of the cabin looking frightened. As if to reassure himself, the boatswain ordered the men about all the more harshly.

Our allowed dozen were to be Rovic, Froad, myself, Etien, and eight crewmen. All were supplied with helmets and corselets, muskets and edged weapons. Since Guzan had told us there was a beaten path to the Ship, we assembled a supply cart on the dock. Etien supervised its lading. I was astonished to see that nearly all it carried, till the axles groaned, was barrels of gunpowder. ''But we're not taking cannon!'' I protested.

''Skipper's orders,'' rapped Etien. He turned his back on me. After a glance at Rovic's face, no one ventured to ask him the reason. I remembered we would be going up a mountainside. A wagonful of powder, with lit fuse, set rolling down toward a hostile army, might win a battle. But did Rovic anticipate open conflict so soon?

Certes his orders to the men and officers remaining behind suggested as much. They were to stay aboard the *Golden Leaper*, holding her ready for instant fight or flight.

As the sun rose, we said our morning prayers to God's Daughter and marched down the docks. The wood banged hollow under our boots. A few thin mists drifted on the bay; Tambur's crescent hung wan above. Nikum Town was hushed as we passed through.

Guzan met us at the temple. A son of Iskilip was supposedly in charge, but the duke ignored that youth as much as we did. They had a hundred guardsmen with them, scaly-coated, shaven-headed, tattooed with storms and dragons. The early sunlight gleamed off obsidian spearheads. Our approach was watched in silence. But when we drew up before those disorderly ranks, Guzan trod forth. He was also y-clad in leather, and carried the sword Rovic had given him on Yarzik. The dew shimmered on his feather cloak. "What have you in that wagon?" he demanded.

"Supplies," Rovic answered.

"For four days?"

"Send home all but ten of your men," said Rovic coolly, "And I'll send back this cart."

Their eyes clashed, until Guzan turned and gave his orders. We started off, a few Montalirians surrounded by pagan warriors. The jungle lay ahead of us, a deep and burning green, rising halfway up the slope of Ulas. Then the mountain became naked black, up to the snow that edged its smoking crater.

Val Nira walked between Rovic and Guzan. Strange, I thought, that the instrument of God's will for us was so shriveled. He ought to have walked tall and haughty, with a star on his brow.

During the day, at night when we made camp, and again the next day, Rovic and Froad questioned him eagerly about his home. Of course, all their talk was in fragments. Nor did I hear everything, since I must take my turn at pulling our wagon along that narrow, upward, damnable trail. The Hisagazi have no draft animals, therefore they make very little use of the wheel and have no proper roads. But what I did hear kept me long awake.

Ah, greater marvels than the poets have imagined for Elf Land! Entire cities built in a single tower half a mile high. The sky made to glow so that there is no true darkness after sunset. Food not grown in the earth, but manufactured in alchemical laboratories. The lowest peasant owning a score of machines which serve him more subtly and humbly than might a thousand slaves—owning an aerial carriage which can fly him around his world in less than a day—owning a crystal window on which theatrical images appear, to beguile his abundant leisure. Argosies between suns, stuffed with the wealth of a thousand planets; yet every ship unarmed and unescorted, for there are no pirates and this realm has long ago come to such good terms with the other starfaring nations that war has also ceased. (These other countries, it seems, are more akin to the supernatural than Val Nira's, in that the races composing them are not human, though able to speak and reason.) In this happy land there is little crime. When it does occur, the criminal is soon captured by the arts of the provost corps; yet he is not hanged, nor even transported overseas. Instead, his mind is cured of the wish to violate any law. He returns home to live as an especially honored citizen, since all know he is now completely trustworthy. As for the government—but here I lost the thread of discourse. I believe it is in form a republic, but in practice a devoted fellowship of men, chosen by examination, who see to the welfare of everyone else.

Surely, I thought, this was Paradise!

Our sailors listened with mouths agape. Rovic's mien was reserved, but he gnawed his mustaches incessantly. Guzan, to whom this was an old tale, grew rough of manner. Plain to see, he disliked our intimacy with Val Nira, and the ease wherewith we grasped ideas that were spoken.

But then, we came of a nation which has long encouraged natural philosophy and improvement of all mechanic arts. I myself, in my short lifetime, had witnessed the replacement of the waterwheel in regions where there are few streams, by the modern form of windmill. The pendulum clock was invented the year before I was born. I had read many romances about the flying machines which no few men have tried to devise.

Living at such a dizzy pace of progress, we Montalirians were well prepared to entertain still vaster concepts.

At night, sitting up with Froad and Etien around a camp fire, I spoke somewhat of this to the savant. "Ah," he crooned, "today Truth stood unveiled before me. Did you hear what the starman said? The three laws of planetary motion about a sun, and the one great law of attraction which explains them? Dear saints, that law can be put in a single short sentence, and yet the development will keep mathematicians busy for three hundred years!"

He stared past the flames, and the other fires around which the heathen men slept, and the jungle gloom, and the angry volcanic glow in heaven. I started to query him. "Leave be, lad," grunted Etien. "Can ye nay tell when a man's in love?"

I shifted my position, a little closer to the boatswain's stolid, comforting bulk. "What do you think of all this?" I asked, softly, for the jungle whispered and croaked on every side.

"Me, I stopped thinking a while back," he said. "After yon day on the quarterdeck, when the skipper jested us into sailing wi' him though we went off the world's edge an' tumbled down in foam amongst the nether stars . . . well, I'm but a poor sailor man, an' our one chance o' regaining home is to follow the skipper."

"Even beyond the sky?"

"Less hazard to that, maybe, than sailing on around the world. The little man swore his vessel was safe, an' that there're no storms between the suns.''

"Can you trust his word?''

"Oh, aye. Even a knocked-about old palomer like me has seen enough o' men to ken when a one's too timid an' eagersome to stand by a lie. I fear not the folk in Paradise, nor does the skipper. Except in some way—'' Etien rubbed his bearded jaw, scowling. "In some way I can nay wholly grasp, they affright Rovic. He fears nay they'll come hither wi' torch an' sword; but there's somewhat else about 'em that frets him.''

I felt the ground shudder, ever so faintly. Ulas had cleared his throat. "It does seem we'd be daring God's anger—''

"That's nay what gnaws on the skipper's mind. He was never an overpious man.'' Etien scratched himself, yawned, and climbed to his feet. "Glad I am to be nay the skipper. Let him think over what's best to do. Time ye an' me was asleep.''

But I slept little that night.

Rovic, I think, rested well. Yet as the next day wore on, I could see haggardness on him. I wondered why. Did he think the Hisagazi would turn on us? If so, why had he come at all? As the slope steepened, the wagon grew so toilsome to push and drag that my fears died for lack of breath.

Yet when we came upon the Ship, toward evening, I forgot my weariness. And after one amazed volley of oaths, our mariners rested si-

lent on their pikes. The Hisagazi, never talk-
ative, crouched low in token of awe. Only Guzan
remained erect among them. I glimpsed his expression as he stared at the marvel. It was a look
of lust.

Wild was that place. We had gone above tim-
berline, so the land was a green sea below us,
edged with silvery ocean. Here we stood among
tumbled black boulders, with cinders and spongy
tufa underfoot. The mountain rose in steeps and
scarps and ravines, up to the snows and the
smoke, which rose another mile into a pale chilly
day. And here stood the Ship.

And the Ship was beauty.

I remember. In length—height, rather, since it
stood on its tail—it was about equal to our own
caravel, in form not unlike a lance head, in color
a shining white untarnished after forty years.
That was all. But words are paltry, my lords.
What can they show of clean soaring curves, of
iridescence on burnished metal, of a thing which
was proud and lovely and in its very shape
aquiver to be off? How can I conjure back the
glamor which hazed that Ship whose keel had
cloven starlight?

We stood there a long time. My vision blurred.
I wiped my eyes, angry to be seen so affected,
until I noticed one tear glisten in Rovic's red
beard. But the captain's visage was quite blank.
When he spoke, he said merely, in a flat voice,
"Come, let's make camp."

The Hisagazian guardsmen dared approach no
closer than these several hundred yards, to so

potent an idol as the Ship had become. Our own
mariners were glad enough to maintain the same
distance. But after dark, when all else was in
order, Val Nira led Rovic, Froad, Guzan, and
myself to the vessel.

As we approached, a double door in the side
swung noiselessly open and a metal gangplank
descended therefrom. Glowing in Tambur's light,
and in the dull clotted red reflected off the smoke
clouds, the Ship was already as strange as I could
endure. When it thus opened itself to me, as if
a ghost stood guard, I whimpered and fled. The
cinders crunched beneath my boots; I caught a
whiff of sulfurous air.

But at the edge of camp I rallied myself enough
to look again. The dark ground blotted all light,
so that the Ship appeared alone with its gran-
deur. Presently I went back.

The interior was lit by luminous panels, cool
to the touch. Val Nira explained that the great
engine which drove it—as if the troll of folklore
were put on a treadmill—was intact, and would
furnish power at the flick of a lever. As nearly
as I could understand what he said, this was done
by changing the metallic part of ordinary salt
into light . . . so I do not understand after all.
The quicksilver was required for a part of the
controls, which channeled power from the engine into another mechanism that hurtled the
Ship skyward. We inspected the broken con-
tainer. Enormous indeed had been the impact of
landing, to twist and bend that thick alloy so.
And yet Val Nira had been shielded by invisible

forces, and the rest of the ship had not suffered important damage. He fetched some tools, which flamed and hummed and whirled, and demonstrated a few repair operations on the broken part. Obviously he would have no trouble completing the work—and then he need only pour in a gallon of quicksilver, to bring his vessel alive again.

Much else did he show us that night. I shall say naught of this, for I cannot even remember such strangeness very clearly, let alone find words. Suffice it that Rovic, Froad, and Zhean spent a few hours in Elf Hill.

So, too, did Guzan. Though he had been taken here once before, as part of his initiation, he had never been shown this much ere now. Watching him, however, I saw less marveling in him than greed.

No doubt Rovic observed the same. There was little which Rovic did not observe. When we departed the Ship, his silence was not stunned like Froad's or my own. At the time, I thought in a vague fashion that he fretted over the trouble Guzan was certain to make. Now, looking back, I believe his mood was sadness.

Sure it is that long after we others were in our bedrolls, he stood alone, looking at the planet-lit Ship.

Early in a cold dawn, Etien shook me awake. "Up, lad, we've work to do. Load yere pistols an' belt on yere dirk."

"What? What's to happen?" I fumbled with a hoarfrosted blanket. Last night seemed a dream.

"The skipper's nay said, but plainly he awaits a fight. Report to the wagon an' help us move into yon flying tower." Etien's thick form heel-squatted a moment longer beside me. Then, slowly: "Methinks Guzan has some idea o' murdering us all, here on the mountain. One officer an' a few crewmen can be made to sail the *Golden Leaper* for him, to Giair an' back. The rest o' us would be less trouble to win wi' our weasands slit."

I crawled forth, teeth clattering in my head. After arming myself, I snatched some food from the common store. The Hisagazi on the march carry dried fish and a sort of bread made from a powdered weed. Only the saints knew when I'd next get a chance to eat. I was the last to join Rovic at the cart. The natives were drifting sullenly toward us, unsure what we intended.

"Let's go, lads," said Rovic. He gave his orders. Four men started manhandling the wagon across the rocky trail toward the Ship, where this gleamed among mists. We others stood by, weapons ready. Almost at once Guzan hastened toward us, with Val Nira toiling in his wake.

Anger darkened his countenance. "What are you doing?" he barked.

Rovic gave him a calm stare. "Why, milord, as we may be here for some time, inspecting the wonders aboard the Ship—"

"What?" interrupted Guzan. "What do you mean? Have you not seen enough for one visit?

43

We must get home again, and prepare to sail after the flowing stone.''

''Go if you wish,'' said Rovic. ''I choose to linger. And since you don't trust me, I reciprocate the feeling. My folk will stay in the Ship, which can be defended if necessary.''

Guzan stormed and raged, but Rovic ignored him. Our men continued hauling the cart over the uneven ground. Guzan signaled his spearmen, who approached in a disordered but alert mass. Etien spoke a command. We fell into line. Pikes slanted forward, muskets took aim.

Guzan stepped back. We had demonstrated firearms for him at his own home island. Doubtless he could overwhelm us with sheer numbers, were he determined enough, but the cost would be heavy. ''No reason to fight, is there?'' purred Rovic. ''I am only taking a sensible precaution. The Ship is a most valuable prize. It could bring Paradise for all . . . or dominion over this earth for one. There are those who'd prefer the latter. I've not accused you of being among them. However, in prudence I'd liefer keep the Ship for my hostage and my fortress, as long as it pleases me to remain here.''

I think then I was convinced of Guzan's real intentions, not as a surmise of ours but as plain fact. Had he truly wished to attain the stars, his one concern would have been to keep the Ship safe. He would not have reached out, snatched little Val Nira in his powerful hands, and dragged the starman backward like a shield against our fire. Not that his intent matters, save to my own conscience. Wrath distorted his patterned visage. He screamed at us, "Then I'll keep a hostage too! And much good may your shelter do you!"

The Hisagazi milled about, muttering, hefting their spears and axes, but not prepared to follow us. We grunted our way across the black mountainside. The sun strengthened. Froad twisted his beard. "Dear me, master captain," he said, "think you they'll lay siege to us?"

"I'd not advise anyone to venture forth alone," said Rovic dryly.

"But without Val Nira to explain things, what use for us to stay at the Ship? Best we go back. I've mathematic texts to consult—my head's aspin with the law that binds the turning planets—I must ask the man from Paradise what he knows of—"

Rovic interrupted with a gruff order to three men, that they help lift a wheel wedged between two stones. He was in a savage temper. I confess his action seemed mad to me. If Guzan intended treachery, we had gained little by immobilizing ourselves in the Ship, where he could starve us. Better to let him attack in the open, where we would have a chance of fighting our way through. On the other hand, if Guzan did not plan to fall on us in the jungle—or any other time—then this was senseless provocation on our part. But I dared not question.

When we had brought our wagon up to the Ship, its gangplank again descended for us. The sailors started and cursed. Rovic forced himself out of his own bitterness, to speak soothing words. "Easy, lads. I've been aboard already, ye ken. Naught harmful within. Now we must tote our powder thither, an' stow it as I've planned."

Being slight of frame, I was not set to carrying the heavy casks, but put at the foot of the gangplank to watch the Hisagazi. We were too far away to distinguish words, but I saw how Guzan stood up on a boulder and harangued them. They shook their weapons at us and whooped. But they did not venture to attack. I wondered wretchedly what this was all about. If Rovic had foreseen us besieged, that would explain why he brought so much powder along . . . no, it would not, for there was more than a dozen men could shoot off in weeks of musketry, even had we had enough lead along . . . and we had almost no food! I looked past the poisonous volcano clouds, to Tambur where storms raged that could engulf all our earth, and wondered what demons lurked here to possess men.

I sprang to alertness at an indignant shout from within. Froad! Almost, I ran up the gangway, then remembered my duty. I heard Rovic roar him down and order the crewfolk to carry on. Froad and Rovic must have gone alone into the pilot's compartment and talked for an hour or more. When the old man emerged, he protested no longer. But as he walked down the gangway, he wept.

Rovic followed, grimmer of countenance than I had ever seen a man ere now. The sailors filed after, some looking appalled, some relieved, but chiefly watching the Hisagazian camp. They were simple mariners; the Ship was little to them save an alien and disquieting thing. Last came Etien, walking backward down the metal plank as he uncoiled a long string.

"Form square!" barked Rovic. The men snapped into position. "Best get within, Zhean and Froad," said the captain. "You can better carry extra ammunition than fight." He placed himself in the van.

I tugged Froad's sleeve. "Please, I beg you, master, what's happening?" But he sobbed too much to answer.

Etien crouched with flint and steel in his hands. He heard me—for otherwise we were all deathly silent—and said in a hard voice: "We placed casks o' powder throughout this hull, lad, wi' powder trains to join 'em. Here's the fuse to the whole."

I could not speak, could not even think, so monstrous was this. As if from immensely far away, I heard the click of stone on steel in Etien's fingers, heard him blow on the spark and add: "A good idea, methinks. I said t'other eventide, I'd follow the skipper wi'out fear o' God's curse—but better 'tis not to tempt Him overmuch."

"Forward march!" Rovic's sword blazed clear of the scabbard.

Our feet scrunched loud and horrible on the mountain as we quick-stepped away. I did not look back. I could not. I was still fumbling in a nightmare. Since Guzan would have moved to intercept us anyhow, we proceeded straight to-

ward his band. He stepped forward as we halted
at the camp's edge. Val Nira slunk shivering after
him. I heard the words dimly:

"Well, Rovic, what now? Are you ready to go
home?"

"Yes," said the captain. His voice was dull.
"All the way home."

Guzan squinted in rising suspiciousness.
"Why did you abandon your wagon? What did
you leave behind?"

"Supplies. Come, let's march."

Val Nira stared at the cruel shapes of our
pikes. He must wet his lips a few times ere he
could quaver, "What are you talking about?
There's no reason to leave food there. It would
spoil in all the time until . . . until—" He fal-
tered as he looked into Rovic's eyes. The blood
drained from him.

"What have you done?" he whispered.

Suddenly Rovic's free hand went up, to cover
his face. "What I must," he said thickly.
"Daughter of God, forgive me."

The starman regarded us an instant more.
Then he turned and ran. Past the astonished warriors he burst, out onto the cindery slope, toward
his Ship.

"Come back!" bellowed Rovic. "You fool
you'll never—"

He swallowed hard. As he looked after that
small, stumbling, lonely shape, hurrying across
a fire mountain toward the Beautiful One, the
sword sank in his grasp. "Perhaps it's best," he
said, like a benediction.

Guzan raised his own sword. In scaly coat and blowing feathers, he was a figure as impressive as steel-clad Rovic. "Tell me what you've done," he snarled, "or I'll kill you this moment!"

He paid our muskets no heed. He, too, had had dreams.

He, too, saw them end, when the Ship exploded.

Even that adamantine hull could not withstand a wagonload of carefully placed gunpowder, set off at one time. There came a crash that knocked me to my knees, and the hull cracked open. White-hot chunks of metal screamed across the slopes. I saw one of them strike a boulder and split it in twain. Val Nira vanished, destroyed too quickly to have seen what happened; so in the ultimate, God was merciful to him. Through the flames and smokes and doomsday noise which followed, I saw the Ship fall. It rolled down the slope, strewing its own mangled guts behind. Then the mountainside grumbled and slid in pursuit, and buried it, and dust hid the sky.

More than this, I have no heart to remember.

The Hisagazi shrieked and fled. They must have thought all hell came to earth. Guzan stood his ground. As the dust enveloped us, hiding the grave of the Ship and the white volcano crater, turning the sun red, he sprang at Rovic. A musketeer raised his weapon. Etien slapped it down. We stood and watched those two men fight, up and over the shaken cinder land, and knew in our private darkness that this was their right.

Sparks flew where the blades clamored together. At last Rovic's skill prevailed. He took Guzan in the throat.

We gave Guzan decent burial and went down through the jungle.

That night the guardsmen rallied their courage enough to attack us. We were aided by our muskets, but must chiefly use sword and pike. We hewed our way through them because we had no other place to go than the sea.

They gave up, but carried word ahead of us. When we reached Nikum, all the forces Iskilip could raise were besieging the *Golden Leaper* and waiting to oppose Rovic's entry. We formed a square again, and no matter how many thousands they had, only a score or so could reach us at any time. Nonetheless, we left six good men in the crimsoned mud of those streets. When our people on the caravel realized Rovic was coming back, they bombarded the town. This ignited the thatch roofs and distracted the enemy enough that a sortie from the ship was able to effect a juncture with us. We chopped our way to the pier, got aboard, and manned the capstan.

Outraged and very brave, the Hisagazi paddled their canoes up to our hull, where our cannon could not be brought to bear. They stood on each other's shoulders to reach our rail. One band forced itself aboard, and the fight was fierce which cleared them from the decks. That was when I got the shattered collarbone which plagues me to this day.

But in the end, we came out of the fjord. A

fresh east wind was blowing. With all sail aloft, we outran the foe. We counted our dead, bound our wounds, and slept.

Next dawning, awakened by the pain of my shoulder and the worse pain within, I mounted the quarterdeck. The sky was overcast. The wind had stiffened; the sea ran cold and green, whitecaps out to a cloud-gray horizon. Timbers groaned and rigging skirled. I stood an hour facing aft, into the chill wind that numbs pain.

When I heard boots behind me, I did not turn around. I knew they were Rovic's. He stood beside me a long while, bareheaded. I noticed that he was starting to turn gray.

Finally, not yet regarding me, still squinting into the air that lashed tears from our eyes, he said: "I had a chance to talk Froad over, that day. He was grieved, but owned I was right. Has he spoken to you about it?"

"No," I said.

"None of us are ever likely to speak of it much," said Rovic.

After another time: "I was not afraid Guzan or anyone else would seize the Ship and try to turn conqueror. We men of Montalir should well be able to deal with any such rogues. Nor was I afraid of the Paradise dwellers. That poor little man could only have been telling truth. They would never have harmed us . . . willingly. They would have brought precious gifts, and taught us their own esoteric arts, and let us visit all their stars."

"Then why?" I got out.

"Someday Froad's successors will solve the riddles of the universe," he said. "Someday our descendants will build their own Ship, and go forth to whatever destiny they wish."

Spume blew up and around us, until our hair was wet. I tasted the salt on my lips.

"Meanwhile," said Rovic, "we'll sail the seas of this earth, and walk its mountains, and chart and subdue and come to understand it. Do you see, Zhean? That is what the Ship would have taken from us."

Then I was also made able to weep. He laid his hand on my uninjured shoulder and stood with me while the *Golden Leaper*, all sail set, proceeded westward.

Steven POPKES

SLOW LIGHTNING

This work is dedicated to the
Cambridge Science Fiction Workshop
now in its tenth year.

The members of the workshop who contributed
most to this work are:

Jon Burrowes
Steven Caine
Resa Nelson
Alex Jablokov
Geoff Landis
David A. Smith
Sara Smith

Without these people this work would never have
been written.

The Egg: 2035 AD

The rusty, pitted steel was soft but sharp as a knife. It was thirty or forty feet back to the beach. I didn't really want to climb back down; I didn't even have to look to convince myself. I knew how far it was. I tried rehearsing things I could say to my Aunt Sara: "Once I got that high, I had to keep going. It was too far to get back down," or "I was just trying to go up a little ways, but then I got stuck." I shook my head. Didn't wash. She'd never *told* me not to come here, but the wreck was the kind of thing she thought eleven-year-old boys Should Not Mess With.

Wasn't my home anyway.

I stretched my neck trying to see over the hull

to the upper deck. I'd seen the wreck with Aunt Sara's binoculars a couple of weeks before. Well, Gray'd seen it and pointed it out to me. *I'd* needed the binoculars, not him. His eyes are a lot sharper than people's eyes. It had taken me a couple of weeks to figure out how to get over here—two condemned bridges and an old mud flat's worth of time.

It was a big ferry, forty meters if it was anything. It was called the *Hesperus*—I'd got that much from my cousin Jack before he decided I was too young to talk to. I stood there and looked at it. The pontoons had of course collapsed and rotted away—the wreck had been there about five or six years. There were broken-all-over tubes like so many snakes. These were the pressure fittings to fill up the pontoons, I think. Some of the blue and white paint was still showing in places on the housings, and where the brass fittings were still there and not all corroded and crumbled by the salt, you could still see a little yellow shine. It must have looked grand, running passengers and cars across the harbor, maybe pulling the whistle at some of the larger ships going up to Maine or over to Europe or Africa—the kind of thing I'd read about happening on earth since I was a little kid.

I heard sort of a whisper from the beach and looked down. It was Mama. She stood on the sand staring at me, eyes frowned and crinkled at the edges, the way mothers get when they're worried. You know. She'd done that even when she was alive.

I said, "You worry too much, Mama." I looked up again. It wasn't that far. I looked back to the ground to tell her that but she was gone. I wished she'd stay in one place for a while.

I kept my balance by holding the edge of a warped hull plate. The ledge was narrow, rotting like an old log, but it carried me over the pontoon housings. The wind blew from inland. It went right through my jacket. Cold. I shivered like I was almost dead—the way the swamp miners shake when they cough back home. Home. That was something. This was supposed to be home, now. All my life I'd heard how good it was going to be on earth. Well, you could have earth as far as I was concerned. It wasn't worth a dog's hind leg to me.

The upper hull wasn't crumbling like the housings, but it was slick from the greasy harbor water. I'd heard tell of the Boston Harbor Cleanup, but I didn't believe in it.

The wreck had two bridge towers. One of the automobile gates had fallen inward, and the other was held up by just one rusty hinge. It was so heavy it didn't move with the wind. But sometimes it made these echoing cracks like gunfire a long way off. Let me tell you, I know what guns sound like.

The inside of the ferry was a hollow cave that smelled like the sea at low tide. You know the smell? I didn't, then. It's like something died and was pickled in gasoline. I followed this dark stairway from the auto bay to the passenger deck. You could see Boston from there, the domes looked like the foggy blue crystal glasses Mama had on the shelf at home. I don't know what happened to them. They must have been auctioned off to pay for my ticket here. Anyway, the high buildings were just a bunch of sticks. I could see the boats just outside of Revere. I shaded my eyes but I couldn't pick out Aunt Sara's.

On the inland side of the wreck, I found a narrow little ladder that looked like it went up to the bridge. It shook some when I started to climb it, but I thought it was okay.

Halfway up, the ladder shifted. I stopped.

"Don't do this to me," I said softly. "I got enough problems."

The ladder creaked again.

"I said don't!"

The old rivets popped out of the hull. I grabbed on as hard as I could. Slow as a dream, the ladder pulled away from the hull and I began to fall. I cried out.

The ladder stopped in midair. I choked on the yell and looked down.

Gray stood below me, two arms holding the ladder, four arms holding the hull, and the remaining two ready to catch me. I grinned and relaxed. "Hey there!" I called down to him.

Gray pushed the ladder back against the hull. "Ira, come down."

"I want to look at the bridge."

"It is not safe."

"You're here, now, right? You're not going to let anything happen to me."

Gray considered for a moment. He didn't move

60

at all when he did that, just still, like a big, gray leather rock. "True. Go to the top of the ladder and stand on the ledge. I will follow."

I climbed to the top and stood away from the edge. Gray ripped the ladder entirely away from the boat and threw it over the side. Then, he leaped the thirty or forty feet to the upper deck and sat down to keep from bumping his head.

When he was alive, Papa described Gray like this:

"Well, he's huge, close to nine feet tall and a quarter ton in weight. You can't think of him as a whole, but only in pieces. Like, he's got the body of a bear but with these overlapping plates of leather of a rhino. His limbs are thick like the legs of an elephant, blunt at the end but with maybe a dozen small fingers, as hard and supple as the legs of a spider. His head is scaled to the rest of him with two wideset eyes and a little mouth in the center, like the face of a buffalo. There are bumps and protrusions around his face that belong to nothing on earth.

"He's not ugly—in fact, he's kind of beautiful—but he's strange."

I don't know whether he's strange or not—I grew up with him and he always looked normal to me. But that part about the animals is right. I looked them up myself.

"This relic is dangerous," he said. "I wish you had invited me."

I looked away and felt a little guilty. "I wanted to see it for myself."

Gray was silent a moment. "Just so. I had

forgotten you are getting older. You must use your own judgment, of course. Should I go?''

I leaned against him. His hard body was cold for a minute, but as I lay there, it grew warmer and softer. Gray was all the home I needed. Which was good, since I didn't have one anymore. "No. It'll be more fun with somebody to talk to." And Aunt Sara wouldn't be able to yell at me. "Let's look at the bridge."

The windows were broken and there were these different sized holes in the boards where the instruments had been. Gray didn't say anything while I looked but followed me down the other side to the passenger compartments. There, the top had caved in and the open space was sunny. Pieces of metal and wire and chain were all over the floor. Old mattresses and rags were piled up against the walls. "Looks like dynamite in a mattress factory," I said and giggled.

"Adolescent parties, perhaps." Gray pointed to one wall. "Look at the graffiti."

I nodded but I wasn't much interested. There was a crazy smell here, sour-sharp like ammonia or lemons. I had never smelled anything like it, and it made me curious. Rags were piled against the bundle of chains in the corner and the smell seemed to come from there. I reached towards the pile and Gray stopped me.

"Wait a moment," said Gray.

I held back. He never did anything without a reason. He's funny that way—not like people, you see. He always knows what he's doing.

He delicately pulled apart the rags. In the center was an egg the size of a basketball.

"Huh." I stared at the egg. It was wrinkled gray, with smears of yellow and red on the sides.

"What kind of egg is it?" I leaned over Gray's arm.

"I have no idea."

"It could be anything!"

Gray nodded.

"It could be dragons. Or griffins." Gray just looked at me. I grinned at him. "Well, okay. It *could* be aliens nobody has ever heard of. It could take us somewhere." Somewhere different. Better.

"The universe is a large place. It could be many things."

"Can we hatch it?"

Gray replaced the rags, then turned to me. "If you wish."

The sun was getting low. I could feel the chill in the wind. The cold might be bad for the egg. Dragons. Griffins. Gray never said there weren't any; just that they were hard to find. "Should we take it back to Aunt Sara's boat? It's going to get cold here."

Gray was silent. "It was put here on purpose. Something thinks this is the best place for it."

That made sense. "I'll come back and check it tomorrow."

Gray stood. "It is getting late. We should go back."

"Okay."

Gray helped me down the side of the wreck and walked beside me. "Ira," he said suddenly.

"Yes."

"Let me come with you when you visit the egg."

I shrugged. You could trust Gray. You could trust him with anything. "All right." We walked on a little further. I felt cold and tired. "Carry me?"

Gray did not answer but picked me up and held me close against his belly with a middle set of arms. Gray's belly grew warm and I got sleepy. For a second, I thought I could hear my mother but it was just a night bird.

"Mama was watching me climb the wreck."

"Did she say anything?"

I shrugged. "No. She was just worried." I liked the feel of Gray's arm, the muscles under the thick leather. Like elephants or rhinos. I'd seen pictures, like I said before. "I miss them."

"I do, too."

I could see Papa walking next to Gray. Then, it got too dark, but I could still hear him walking. I felt sad and sleepy and about to cry. "Papa?"

I don't think he heard me, but in a minute he began to sing:

I dreamed I saw Joe Hill last night,
alive as you and me.
I said, "Joe Hill you're ten years dead."
"I never died," said he.

He used to sing that to me at night, when I couldn't sleep.

Gray was quiet. I snuggled deep into his arms. I felt warm and safe and I didn't feel I had to cry for a while. Pretty soon, I fell asleep.

Damn.

Sara Monahan hated boats.

Boats wobbled, wiggled, and writhed to the beating of the sea. Boats were dirty. Boats smelled.

She cut the motor in the whaler and let it drift the last five or six meters to the dock. It was time enough for her to light a cigarette and cough, ready the line and toss it over the cleat on the dock and pull the whaler in. She didn't think about it. Sara Monahan had been a boat person all her life. She'd been conceived and born on a boat. She'd grown up the daughter of a fisherman, grown into a young girl in the flooded city of Hull, amidst the squalor of *that* place. Sara shuddered at the memory. She'd never blamed the police when they bombed Lat Do, just her father when he wouldn't leave and her mother for siding with him.

They'd never made it out of the firestorm.

She'd dragged Roni wailing to the whaler and gunned the ancient motor, praying it wouldn't die, and gotten out just ahead of the police fighters. Sara and Roni had kept watch at the casualty lists in the refugee camps for nearly a year just in case. Nothing.

Screw Boston. Screw the police.

They'd made their way to Revere and lived on their inheritance: the *Hercules*. Sara had scraped by, studying for the welding certification exams and started working laying steel in the new building boom. Roni had boned up on the merchant marine and had emigrated as soon as she had passed. They'd barely written to each other for ten years.

Christ.

She looked up suddenly. It was nearly sunset. Never get anywhere if she kept thinking like this. She smelled her singed hair and the burnt metal on her jacket. A shower. She thought about Roni and Roni's kid: Ira. And Ira's nanny: Gray.

She groaned and got out on the dock. It rocked—lord how she hated things that rocked. She boarded and clambered inside the *Hercules*. Sara threw her mask into a chair and leaned against the hull, waiting to see in the gloom. Nobody here. You could tell an empty boat. Something in the way it moved.

There was a grubby note from her son, Jack, that he'd gone to Kendall's for the night. Great. First a long drink, *then* shower. She coughed again. A photograph on the wall attracted her attention. It was Roni and her husband, Gilbert, on their wedding day. Sara opened the bottle and stared at the picture for a long minute. Gilbert was a little fat and wore glasses.

She upended the bottle and took a long drink, turned back to the photograph.

"I have better taste in men than you do, honey," she said to Roni. "Look at that guy. I've seen better faces on kitchen doors."

But mine stayed, her sister seemed to answer. *He didn't leave me pregnant with a son. Where is Mike now?*

"God knows, Roni." Sara drank some more from the bottle. "But when he touched you, you remembered it. Could you say the same?"

Roni didn't answer.

Just as well. If Roni could still talk, the first thing Sara would have asked was: where did she dig Gray up?

"Sara?"

"I'm not here." She stared at Roni. How come you look so miserably happy? You're dead.

"It's Sam."

Sam?

"Sam!" She capped the bottle and looked out on deck. There he was, little and bald and bearded. "Damn you for a fish. Sam! I haven't seen you all summer."

Sam grinned at her. "Been out to George's Bank, fishing. Just got in this morning. Came over to see how you were."

"We're fine." She grabbed his hand and pulled him inside. "You're just in time to save me from drinking alone."

One eyebrow cocked at her. "A young woman like you drinking alone? Shameful. I'll have to help. I'm civilized. I need a coffee cup to drink from."

"Bless you." She laughed.

They sat at the galley table, the bottle between them.

Sam nodded towards the dock. "Where is everybody? It's all empty slips."

Sara shrugged. "Looking for work, mostly. I was lucky to get a job in town. Most of them took off for Marblehead or Quincy—some new buildings, some dock work." Sara was almost giddy with the drinks she'd had earlier and with seeing Sam. "It's good to see you. I've been here mostly by myself this summer. Me and the kids."

Again, the eyebrow. "Kids? Have you been naughty?"

She grinned at him. "Hardly." Then, she remembered and the smile left her. "It's bad news, Sam. It happened while you were away. My sister and her husband—well, they got caught in one of the union riots on Maxwell Station." Sara smiled faintly and shrugged. "Her kid and his—nanny, I guess—came to live with me."

Sam took her hands. "Sara. I am so sorry."

"Yeah." She turned back in to the galley. "It happens all the time, right? To other people." Sara shook her head. "I still can't believe it, you know? It's been months but I keep expecting them to show up." She lifted a hand and let it fall, helplessly. She shrugged and looked at him, gripped his hands hard. "But it's good to see you, Sam."

They shared the bottle.

Sam looked around. "Where are they?"

Sara scratched her hair. To hell with a shower.

It was worth it to see Sam. She lit a cigarette from her previous one. Sam watched her without comment. "Jack's over at Kendall's staying the night. Ira's out with Gray."

"His nanny?"

She giggled. "Yeah. Nine feet tall and looks like a rhino with eight legs. My sister got Ira an *alien* nanny."

"Jesus."

He looked owllike with the twilight reflecting off his big eyes.

"Jesus," he said again. "It must have been crazy on Maxwell Station."

"Crazy enough to kill them both."

"Don't talk that way."

She took the bottle and killed the last of the rum. "You don't know what it's like. I—Roni was my sister. She went off and we didn't talk much, but still—now, she's gone off and got herself killed."

Sam shrugged. "It was pretty bad there. I read they had something called rotlung—"

She ignored him. "So I get this stupid telex from the staff at Maxwell Station that Gilbert and Roni had died in the 'disturbances.' I had to claim their bodies. I had to sign for them like a goddamn parcel post. And for Ira. And for Gray. And then, the funeral." Gray hulking over the mourners, always seeming to reproach her. Ira huddled against his legs, taking comfort. The tears started to fall down her face. "I'd a'sent him packing. But he's in the will. Do you understand that? I have to keep him or I don't get

Roni and Gilbert's estate." She shrugged. "Not much, anyway. But it's a little bit."

Sam reached across the table and took her hand. She stopped as if struck. What am I talking about? She smiled at him, embarrassed, and shook her head. "I'm a little drunk, Sam."

"Hush, Sara. It's all right."

She suddenly realized she was crying and wiped her face in her hands. "Jesus, Sam. I'm sorry."

Sam sat in shadow now. She could only see the faint shine of his eyes. "It's all right."

They were silent a long minute, then Sara withdrew her hand. "Know anything about aliens, Sam?"

"Not a thing."

She stood up and got them both glasses of soda. Enough drinking for a bit. Sam didn't protest.

"Well." She sipped the soda. The bubbles tickled her nose and she had to stop herself from sneezing. "Gray's a spatien. I haven't been able to find out much about them. They're supposed to be great workers, but they don't hang around much in this neck of the woods. Not enough work, I guess. All I know about Gray is that Roni and Gilbert found him somewhere out there, and now he's theirs."

Sam shrugged. "I don't know anything about it. There are lots of aliens in Boston, though. They're all cleared and called safe, anyway. Gray must be cleared, too."

"I suppose. I wish I knew more about him."

Sam smiled at her. "Roni trusted him with her kid. That's something."

Sara nodded.

Sam opened his mouth to speak but they heard a heavy tread on the dock. In a moment, the *Hercules* shuddered as Gray stepped on board. He was carrying Ira, asleep. The cabin was so low he had to shift Ira up to his top set of arms and walk in on the lower three sets to fit.

"He's asleep," Gray said quietly.

Sara nodded. The bottle was out and she felt in the wrong, as she always did in front of Gray. When Gray took Ira into the boys' room she opened the port and tossed the bottle out into the water. It was stupid, but it made her feel better.

Gray came back out into the little galley. "Is there anything for me to do?" he said in a low-pitched rumble.

"No," she whispered. Why was she always whispering? "No," she said more loudly. "Where you been all day?"

"We investigated a wreck near here."

A wreck. "Christ. You were looking at the *Hesperus*? That thing's twenty years old. It's dangerous. I wouldn't let my own kid go there. Nor Ira. You leave that thing alone. You hear me?"

"I hear you." Gray nodded slowly and went back outside. They heard him make his way to the bow and lie down.

Sam and Sara looked at each other for a minute or more.

"Ah, I see," said Sam. "Well, it's not like it's anything Jack didn't do, too."

"I know. But with the two of them out there—it's scary. It's been like that all summer." Roni, she thought. Poor Roni, though it was obscure to her why she felt sorry for Roni, whether it was because she was dead or because she had lived with Gray.

"Look," began Sam, "my dock's all filled with strangers. People from New York and Jersey. Let me come over here—you wouldn't be so alone and I wouldn't be surrounded by strangers."

She looked at him. It was like the breath of home to her. "Sam, I would like that."

"Good. I'll be here tomorrow." He stood up. "I have to go—got a new job tomorrow."

She nodded sleepily to him, stood, and followed him to the dock. She called good-bye to him.

When she turned around, the moon had risen. She saw Gray was dark and motionless against the silvered deck, the shrouds and lines like so much spiderwebbing. Sara passed by him and he did not stir.

Mama was sitting next to my bed when I woke up. She touched my forehead and that startled me awake. "Hi," she said softly. "How are you feeling?"

"Lonely. I went out to the wreck because of that. Were you very worried?"

"Not too much. Gray was there."

"Yeah." I rubbed my eyes. "Are you coming back soon?"

"I can't come back. You know that."

"You're here, aren't you?"

She smiled at me and didn't answer. I smiled back a little bit. I couldn't help it when she did that.

"I miss you." I felt like I wanted to cry again.

"I miss you, too. Are you being a good boy like I told you? How is Gray?"

I wasn't sure so I just shrugged. "You know how he is. It's hard to tell what he's thinking."

"What do you think he's thinking?"

"I don't know." I shrugged again. "I don't think he likes Aunt Sara. She doesn't like him."

"Oh." She looked thoughtful. "You be sure you take care of Gray."

"Mama." I grinned at her. "Gray takes care of me! You have to come back to take care of him."

"I told you. I can't. Will you take care of him?"

It didn't seem like that was the way it would be, but I was willing. "Okay."

Then she was gone and Aunt Sara knocked at the door.

"Honey?" Aunt Sara opened the door and looked inside. "Were you talking to somebody?"

She coughed like Mama. For a moment, it was almost as if Mama had come back for good. But I smelled the cigarette smoke instead of the sweet swamp smell and knew it was just Aunt Sara coughing from that and not Mama coughing up like she did just before bed, back home. I didn't want to talk to her right then. So I pretended I was asleep. I could see she watched me for a long time, then closed the door and went off to bed herself.

Jack came back early in the morning before she left. He was a quick boy, slick in his movements, getting by on a wink and a grin. He was easy about most things. Sara watched him as he came on the dock towards the *Hercules*, whistling. She couldn't help grinning. Mike had been exactly the same way: wild Irish good looks, a quick grin. When he had touched her . . .

She shook her head. Mike had left fourteen years ago.

"Hey, Ma."

"Hey, kid. How was Kendall?"

"Okay. Got any food around here?"

She nodded. "Gray still outside?"

"I didn't check." He rummaged around in a cupboard and brought out an apple. "When are we going to get rid of that creep?"

"Don't talk about him that way."

Jack stared at the ceiling and rolled his eyes. Sara laughed, looked at the clock. "Christ. I've got to get to work. You take care, now."

Sara grabbed her welding helmet from the hook on the door and dashed down the dock. As she reached the whaler, there was an eruption of water next to it. She stifled a scream and backed away.

Gray held onto the dock and looked up at her. "Sorry."

"Christ on a stick." She stepped into the whaler. "What the hell are you doing here?"

"Repairing the dock."

"Christ on a stick!" She gunned the motor and shot away towards Boston.

The Citibank building was not even half done; there were another three hundred stories to go.

The wind howled through the steel I-beams like a wolf. She grinned as she walked over the girders to the corner where she had left her torch. Over them, the crane crouched spiderlike. It served as crane, resting space, and the building's spine all at once. When the building's frame was finished, the top of the crane—the cab, pulleys, and gears—would be dismantled and shipped to another site. The crane's frame would remain forever part of the building. Her part of the job, welding the I-beams into place, would be finished in a month or so: the steel only went to the hundred and fiftieth floor. After that, it would be composites.

She liked being up here, building the bare bones of the building. People had been building and tearing down in Boston forever. Fitzpatrick, the union boss, was the seventh Fitzpatrick in the steelman's union. Christ, she thought. What must that feel like? Your father, your grandfather, every Fitzpatrick stretching back towards the Civil War. Maybe further. It was like a long chain—God! She'd love that feeling, to be tied to a family like that, to have brothers and uncles and sisters—

"Hey, Sara!"

Sara was so startled she almost lost her balance, something that hadn't happened to her in ten years. She turned and saw Sam walking across the girders towards her. "*This* is your new job?" she cried.

"You bet!"

"Great!"

He winked at her as he looped a safety line over the far corner. Sam held thumb and forefinger together and waved it to her, then pulled himself up over the top support beam.

Maybe her luck was changing. She leaned against a corner and looked down on Boston. It was a bright, sunny day. The light was broken and refracted and reflected by so many glass buildings it was hard to see exactly where the sun was. She liked the crazy quilt mirrors around her. Maybe Sam would like it, too.

Fitzpatrick shouted over to them and pointed down. Below them, the first I-beam of the shift was being brought up from the street. A few men with sledgehammers made ready to pound it in when it reached them. Sam moved away towards the crane team where he was working. She smiled after him and cranked up the torch.

Jack was still in the kitchen when I got up. He grunted when I came out. I didn't like him much. I guess he felt the same way. He reminded me of the supervisor's kids back home. They always looked like they could get anything they wanted. They were always clean—or if they got dirty, it was something that washed off. Not like that gray gunk that made up the marsh around the station. It took alcohol to get that stuff off and then the smell made you sick. They stayed on the board-walk. We stayed in the marsh. That was the way it was.

I only remember the Station. Gray tells me he and Papa and Mama were living on the platform that orbits Maxwell Station when I was two or three, but we couldn't get enough work. I was frozen. That was where the crew found Gray. He and Mama hit it off from the first—Papa, too. The work got better for a while, then it went bust. Sometime after that, they thawed me out and we moved down on the Station. My first memories are of the marsh.

Papa always said what a bad place it was. And it was, I guess. It was wet all the time, and there were slugs the size of your head that would take a bite out of you if you weren't careful. The air was different, too. It seemed you could never get quite enough to breathe—though everybody said the air was just fine. One thing you can say about earth: the air is good.

But the station was good, too. You could get away from people in the marsh. You could fish and swim. It was quiet—here there's always this kind of a rumble from the city.

Anyway, Jack didn't say anything to me when I got up. He barely moved out of my way when I went out on deck to look for Gray. I wanted to tell him not to say anything about the wreck. Gray's good, but he won't keep a secret unless you tell him. He's dumb that way.

He wasn't on deck and I didn't see him around the *Hercules* so I went back inside.

"Have you seen Gray anywhere?" I tried to be polite.

Jack didn't say anything. He yanked open the refrigerator and pulled out some milk.

"Did you hear me?"

"I heard you. I'm not deaf."

"Have you seen him?"

He looked at me. "I don't know where the creep is."

At home, I'd have gone for him right then. But at home nobody'd ever thought to call Gray a creep. I didn't belong here. I never did. I never will.

He looked at me like I was a bug. "You're a creep, too. Why don't you leave? Huh? Asshole. I want my fucking life back. Leave us—we were okay until you got here."

I wanted to cry. "Maybe I will," I shouted and ran out of the boat, across the dock, and into the marsh. After a while, I slowed down. Pretty soon, I didn't want to cry so much.

It at least looked more like home here. I remembered the egg and I started to head over towards the wreck.

I was halfway there before I remembered my promise. I mean, I hadn't said "I promise" to Gray, but it was still a promise. That was the thing: Gray knew what he meant when he asked me, and I knew what he meant when I answered.

I stopped in the middle of some soft ground and sat on a rock. I didn't have any place to go. I felt kind of lost and miserable.

Pretty soon, Papa came and sat down beside me. I would have hugged him but I was afraid he'd disappear. He wasn't as solid about being there as Mama.

"I think I'll run off," I said.

He sighed and leaned on his knees, pushed his glasses against his nose like he always did when he was thinking. He did the same thing that night Boss Skald said they were going to strike.

"You can't leave your family," he said.

"Family!" I picked up a stick and scratched the ground. "They don't want me. I never saw them before this summer."

"Still, they're your family now. Family's got to take you in when you got nowhere else to go." He coughed and turned away from me to spit something on the ground.

I looked at the ground. "I want you and Mama back." I stood up and walked away from him a little. "Why'd you have to go and get killed?"

"It had to be done, Ira. There were reasons—"

"*Family!* You and Mama ran off and left me with Gray. Family."

"Ira—"

"Gray's all the family I got."

I turned around and he was gone. There was nothing there but wind.

"I'm sorry," I said softly. "I didn't mean it."

I waited there for a long time, but he didn't come back.

Sam was painting the front deck when she drew the whaler along the dock. "Hey," she called out to him.

"Yo!" Sam leaned over the railing. "You got a little trouble brewing."

She brought the whaler close to him so he could speak softly. "With Gray?"

He shook his head. "Don't think so. Between Jack and Ira. Ira left this morning, running like hell was after him—angry, you understand. Came back about an hour ago dragging his tail. Sad little kid. The big guy hasn't been around all day."

"Hm."

"I think—" he looked up quickly at her and back at the water, a little embarrassed grimace on his face "—Jack doesn't take too kindly to Ira."

Sara pondered that. "I should get home," she said abruptly.

"Yeah, I've got to finish the forward deck before it gets too cold for the paint to dry." He left the railing and she could hear him whistling a quiet, mournful tune.

She tied up the whaler and walked down the dock towards their slip. She was still a good distance away when she heard a slap and Ira crying. Jack was shouting something unintelligible. There was an eruption of water next to the boat and Gray was suddenly standing on the deck. He moved inside faster than anything had a right to move. Sara started to run.

From the deck she heard Gray's voice: "Stop talking like that."

"How come, creep? Huh?" Jack shouted.

She stopped outside. There was a short pause.

"Because you are torturing someone you love," said Gray.

There was no sound for perhaps a minute, then Jack began sobbing and she ran inside.

"What's going on?" she cried. Jack ran to her and buried his face against her. "Did he hurt you? Jack! What's going on?"

Gray was motionless. Ira looked at Gray, then back at Sara.

Jack pulled back from her and she could see the mark of a slap on the side of his face. "Did Gray do this to you?" she said quietly.

Jack didn't answer.

"If you hurt my son," she said to Gray. Her voice was low and terrible. "If you ever touch my son . . . I'll hurt you."

"I did it," said Ira. His face was white but calm.

She looked at Jack. "Is that true?"

Jack nodded.

"Why?"

Ira put his hands in his pockets and hunched his shoulders. "He called Gray a creep. It wasn't the first time."

She looked at Ira, then back to Jack, then back

to Ira. Finally, she turned to Gray. "I still meant what I said."

"I know," said Gray.

Gray and I were gone the next day before sunup. I was ready to run off right then. I was ready to run off after dinner, but Gray said it wasn't right. I told him about what Papa had said, and he said remember the three loves. Hell, I said, he'd been drilling me with that spatien stuff since I could talk. You shouldn't abandon your family, he said.

It was that kind of conversation.

Family.

On the way to the wreck, Gray didn't say anything. I didn't know what he was thinking, but I could tell he was thinking pretty hard about something. I guessed it was about Sara and Jack.

The egg was nearly twice as big as it had been yesterday, and the smears were gone. Whatever it was, it had to have something better inside it than this. I began to think about what it could be. Gray was no help. He wouldn't even guess what it was. It always makes me mad, the way he won't guess anything. He only says things when he knows the answer to them, and what's the fun of that?

The egg was even more pretty now, with speckles of gold and silver, and the gray had begun to turn to a light blue. Whatever was inside of it had to be beautiful, too. I was still thinking of griffins and dragons, but if it wasn't either of them, it was probably something strange and unusual. I began to think about selling it. With the money, maybe we could buy a ticket out of here. Even Maxwell Station was better than this.

I helped Gray replace the rags over the egg, then the two of us sat on the edge of the wreck, watching the ocean.

"I still want to run off," I said.

"You want your family back," he said.

It almost made me cry I felt so lonesome. He always did this to me, just when I thought I had things figured out, he'd say something true like that and it'd bust everything up.

"Do you remember the three loves?" he said quietly.

I'd known that since I could talk. "Again? Love of family, love of work, love of duty."

"Just so," he murmured. "And always in that order."

I shrugged, having a feeling I wasn't going to like what followed. But he didn't say anything more, just looked out to sea for a long time.

"I have to go to Miller's Hall on Friday. Do you want to come?" he said finally.

Go to Aliens' Hall? Was he serious? "Sure." I was hot to go.

Gray nodded. "Just so. We will leave close to dawn. Can you be up that early?"

You bet I could.

Sam was standing on top of the beam, a safety line leading from him to the crane cable above him. He was so little, Sara thought. But it

83

seemed no hardship for him to use the fourteen-pound sledgehammer. He lifted it high in the air and brought it down on the edge of the beam. The beam rang like a great steel bell and edged another quarter inch between the two framing girders.

He was much stronger than he looked.

He suddenly smiled at her and she started, realizing how closely she had been watching him.

"Hey, lady," he called down to her softly. Sam leaned back over the edge of the girder, looking from one end to the other. He pulled himself back on top and walked to the other end and again lifted the hammer. Bells rang among the towers.

She lit a cigarette, watching the gulls fly down below them.

"Okay, check your end."

Sara nodded and pulled herself up to the edge of the framing girder and measured the angle. "Okay here."

"Weld that sucker."

She pulled down the mask and lit her torch. Three spot welds to hold the end, then up with the mask and she walked the beam to the other side. Three more spot welds.

"Come on down so I can get the rest." She grinned up at him, took a drag on the cigarette. He smiled and danced off the beam like a leprechaun.

Later, at noon, he brought his lunchbox over to her and they ate, watching the sunlight reflect between the buildings.

"You know what I like about Fridays," he said finally.

"No. What?"

He rubbed his hands together maniacally. "Payday. I can buy the *world*."

She laughed. "Hardly. Not on these wages."

Sam shrugged. "Well, it's my first payday." He looked away towards the harbor. "Say, how about dinner?"

"Dinner?" It was as if a sudden wind blew through her. The air did not grow colder but it seemed closer to her skin. "What do you mean?"

"I don't know." He poured himself a cup of coffee from the thermos. "It's been a long summer. I've been out on the Bank, you've been here. I could use the company—do you know what it's like to talk about fishing for three months?"

She laughed and felt relieved and a little disappointed. "I have to go home tonight, though. The kids would worry if I didn't show up."

"Gray could take care of them."

"Gray." She started putting the remains of her lunch back into the lunchbox. "I don't want him around my kids when I can help it."

"Hey." He reached out and touched her arm.

Sara looked at him. He was smiling. "That was a joke," he said gently.

"Yeah." She smiled a little. "Not much of a joke."

"So I'm brain damaged. Three months with the fishing fleets'll do that to you."

"Well," she said slowly, "I still can't go out tonight. I got to get home."

He didn't say anything for a long minute and Sara suddenly wanted to stroke his cheek, feel the smooth skin laid over with a light bristle. A man's cheek. It had been a long time since she had touched a man's skin. Or a woman's skin. Just hugs and touching with Jack or Ira. But not the touching between—

"You could come over to my boat for dinner tonight," he said. His eyes were bright and his munchkin face was crinkled with a silent laughter.

She couldn't help grinning. "Are you going to make me dinner?"

"You bet." He rubbed his hands together. "Got some bluefish I brought back and some snapper. I know a guy on the pier I can trade with for lobster. If you don't like that, I can get—"

Sara touched his arm and he stopped, looked at her hand, then at her.

"Is that a yes?" he said.

"Christ. You— Christ." She threw up her hands. "Dinner. Now, let's work before Fitzpatrick fires us both."

Miller's Hall is named after this guy that first saw the aliens when they landed at Provincetown. Well, they didn't really land there. Some came out of the ship and asked directions to Boston. That's the way the story goes. Gray said it was a little different. He says they weren't really sure what was going on and whatever they asked those people might have sounded like asking for directions, but wasn't that at all. Anyway, Miller is the guy's name.

We caught a ride with Kendall to Wellington Station and took the subway into town.

I'd never been downtown before. Miller's Hall sits across the street from the North End—where the Old North Church is. Gray told me about it and this guy name Paul Revere who carried these lights all across the towns, giving people fire. Up the other street from it is the old Customs House. Gray said it was also called the Gateway to the West. I'd never read anything like this, but maybe he'd read something I hadn't.

The building itself was designed by the aliens so it doesn't look like people ought to live in it. Some do, though. I met a few. One side looks kind of melted, and the other shoots way up above the other in this sharp pointed tower. It's a big place, most of a city block and maybe thirty or forty stories tall. There's a bigger diplomatic building out past Long Wharf in the harbor. It's huge, maybe two hundred stories or something. But it's for big meetings and things. Miller's Hall is where the aliens rest.

While we were coming in on the subway, I tried to get Gray to tell me what we were doing here. He wouldn't tell me, just made that buzzing noise he makes when he doesn't want to answer a question.

"Well," I said, exasperated, "is it about the egg? At least tell me that."

He stopped and picked me up so I was looking at him straight in the eye. He didn't say anything for a minute and I began to get scared. Gray'd never acted that way before. He suddenly looked so *different* from me. I began to think maybe I should have stayed on the *Hercules*.

"Ira. Do you trust me?" he said in a very quiet voice.

"Sure." I shrugged.

"This is very important. Do not mention this thing at all today. Not on the street. Not in this building. Not on the train. Not on the boat home. Nowhere. Not until I say you can. Do you understand me?" Papa was behind him nodding.

That made me mad, both of them ganging up on me like that. "Then why didn't you leave me home if things are so secret."

He didn't say anything for a minute. "We are finding out information. Some information may have something to do with the egg. Some may not. It is useless to speculate. But because we, together, are hatching the egg, this concerns you. You have a right to be here."

"Okay, okay." I punched him on the shoulder. "Okay, already. Don't go formal on me."

"You still don't understand." He paused. "It is important you don't speak here. I do not know how to threaten or persuade you. I can only ask. More: do not display any untoward knowledge. You know my language, you know Common—this I have taught you. Hide that."

He put me down and we went inside.

The lounge had ten or twenty aliens of weird

types. None of them paid much attention to us—I guess we weren't any weirder to them than they were to us. But the place looked strange to me. I mean it was all windows on all four sides, big windows, looking out over the harbor from maybe ten or twenty meters up. I looked back out the door we came in and it was glass and showed the street.

"What are these window things. Holograms?" I asked.

Gray shook his head. "No. They are windows." He looked at them a moment, then turned his head back to me. "N-space was used in the construction of Miller's Hall."

A little alien, shorter than me, came stalking over to me. He stood up at me, all shrunk up and deformed looking, wrinkled brown skin and these *big* blue eyes, swearing a blue streak. Finally, he calmed down enough to stare at me. "What are you staring at?" he said finally, in English.

I started to get mad again, but I remembered what I promised Gray.

"Nothing," I said.

He humphed and hawed a minute. "Nothing. Nothing, he says. Nothing." He put his face almost nose to nose with me and all I could see was those blue eyes.

"Nothing. Tell me, runt, do *you* believe in fairies."

"No," I muttered.

"*Hah!*" he yelled and jumped back, laughing

and clapping his hands. "A smart one! Hah!" He walked off, clapping his hands.

I looked up at Gray and he looked down at me.

"What is that?" I asked.

"Don't worry. He likes you," Gray said.

"How can you tell?" I reached over and grabbed one of his lower legs and held it. I felt nervous all of a sudden.

"He didn't eat you, did he?"

I looked up at him and he just stared back. I punched him hard on the leg. That was Gray's idea of a joke. Like his name. All spatiens are gray. No spatien had a human name until Gray. Naming himself something special with a name that all spatiens could use was Gray's idea of a joke. This was the same.

It made me mad that he'd make a joke now, when ten minutes before he was warning me to keep quiet. Then I figured out that Gray was trying to make me feel better, from what he had talked with me about outside. Maybe he'd even set it up. I punched him again on the leg.

We took a long elevator up into the pointed part of the hall. Up here you could see all the islands, the different buildings out in the harbor, all the hovercraft. I looked down into the city and saw all the Back Bay canals, all with these little boats and canoes going down like people walking down streets. Gray was watching me.

"A hundred years ago, they were streets, not canals."

"Jeez." I shook my head. "What happened?"

"Boston sank. It's still sinking. Before that it was water again. They dumped landfill into the river and made Back Bay. When the *Mayflower* first came to America, Boston was nearly an island." He pointed to the water in Back Bay, and the walls around the inner city ring. "The walls follow the contours of the original Boston." He paused. "The borders are being recycled."

He stared at me and I wrinkled my nose at him. "Ha. Ha. Some joke."

Gray shrugged and led me away from the windows through a long corridor. Again, there were windows on both sides; one side showed the harbor, the other showed the city. It was a different angle now, looking down on the streets with the big buildings, the old Customs House, things like that.

In the next room, there were just two opposite walls made of windows, both looking out on the same section of the harbor. This made me dizzy. I could see the same gulls flying on opposite sides of the room.

"Are *these* holograms?" I asked, not looking at either of them.

"No. Just windows."

The room had a high ceiling like an auditorium. On the floor there was a thick carpet and big pillows where there were various kinds of aliens—too many to keep track of. It was like in one of those bird zoos—aviaries, that's the word—where there are forty or fifty kinds of birds and they move around and are these specks of color, some of them standing still and looking around, some of them hiding, a whole bunch of them shooting over you like bullets. But they aren't all that separate. They're all blurred together. The only way you can tell them apart is by staring hard at the ones that stand still, reading the little descriptions, and wait for the ones that are going like fire over you, hoping like hell you've remembered the names right. You just forget the ones that are hiding.

Well, I didn't have any descriptions.

I saw the little guy that had bugged me in the lounge walking around the sides, kind of watching me from the edge of the crowd.

We walked up to this one pillow and sat down. No one paid us much attention and we sat there for maybe ten minutes. I was getting fidgety.

"What do we do now?"

"We wait here."

"For what?" Maybe Gray had something planned.

"I am not sure."

That was all I could get out of him. He wouldn't even guess—spatiens are like that. They never talk about anything unless it's right there. A pain.

A couple of minutes later Gray began to rub my shoulders the way he does and I got relaxed and a little sleepy, so I leaned against him and he was real warm. I fell asleep like somebody clubbed me.

I dreamed about Papa. He was trying to tell

me something but I couldn't hear him. It was like he was a long way away. He was all agitated and excited and nervous. He kept calling to me, and even though he was only across the room I couldn't hear him. I woke up and there was a kind of buzzing in the room. I sat up and looked around and saw a lot of the aliens looking towards the other door—the other door from where Gray and I had come in, that is. Through the other door was this Centaur—that's what they're called. Not like the Greek myths, you understand. This wasn't half a man, half a horse. This was more like the body of a sow bug and the forward body of a praying mantis—like he was made of sharp points. All but his eyes. His eyes were big and insectoid, a hundred little eyes with slit pupils like a cat's.

He came in the room, moving jerky—at first I thought there was something wrong with him. Then, I saw it was like he was in freeze-frame motion. He didn't move smoothly, but in little jumps like a snapshot. I looked closer and saw I could just barely see him move between those freeze-frames. He'd stop, look down at somebody—he must have been nearly three meters tall—somebody on his other side would speak to him, and suddenly he'd be turned to them. He was so fast it almost made me sick to watch him.

He sidled along the wall, talking to people. The whole room was watching him. It came to me, then, that he was moving towards us, stalking us, almost. With those wicked-looking hands. It made me shake. I looked up at Gray.

He was watching the Centaur. I'd never seen him watch anything so close, even me.

Finally, the Centaur came near us, looked up and saw us both, but acted like he'd only seen Gray. He straightened up and came over to us. "Old-one-of-many-names," he said in Common. "I did not know you were here."

Gray made kind of a half squat-bow, never taking his eyes off the Centaur. "Holy One, I, myself, can barely believe my good fortune."

The Centaur leaned back against his lower half like an old man sitting down in an armchair. "It has been a long time since I have seen you. I have not seen a member of your family since we destroyed that nest—half a cycle ago? Perhaps a full cycle? Are you the last?"

Again, Gray made the half bow. "I do not think I am the last, Holy One. I estivated for almost two cycles before I was found. This was due to the destruction of my nest."

"Ah." The Centaur raised his hand and let it fall like a shrug. "Of course. Is this your pet?" he said looking at me for the first time.

I was almost crazy with nervousness, trying not to look like I knew anything, crazy to find out this thing had killed Gray's family. I wished I had a rifle, a laser, something. It wouldn't have done any good. You could see up close that he spent most of his time waiting for us to catch up. His attention was wandering all around the room. Sharp, though. Damned sharp. I just did my best to look stupid.

"It is no pet, holy one. It is my nephew."

"Are you certain?" The Centaur put one arm on the other like a man folding his arms, but this looked like he was getting ready for something. I almost cried out. *He knows, Gray. He knows. Let's get* out *of here.*

"I am certain, holy one. How are your offspring?"

The Centaur looked up at him and I breathed a little easier. "Fine. I brought two pupa with me and they will be molting soon. No eggs as yet. Pity, as I have been hungering for a delicacy a great deal. But it would be a shame to return home with no children so I have restrained myself. Soon, though, they will molt and of course become children. Tell me: do you think I would be too shamed by returning with only one child?"

"You have no eggs, holy one?"

"None as yet. I have tried several times but the flesh will not obey me." The Centaur turned his head all the way around behind him, watching something for a quick moment and then brought it back again with a snap. I wanted to throw up. "Give me the pupa you have. It would be well cooked. Look"—he pointed to me. "It does not even know Common."

"I cannot, holy one."

"Come. Give it to me as a present." He stiffened somehow and looked like a whip caught in midair.

I heard a soft sound from Gray and turned towards him. He'd extended every finger on every arm and each one grew a razor.

"I cannot, Holy One," he said softly. "Forgive me."

They stared at each other for some minutes, then the Centaur relaxed. "It is a very great sin. But perhaps the fault is mine. I encourage my appetites as much as I can. Perhaps that is not always a virtue." His head snapped around and back again. He looked at me for what felt like an hour, then turned back to Gray. "I must go, my friend. Until we meet again."

He turned and moved away as smoothly as if he'd been on wheels.

"What's going on?" I whispered to Gray.

"Hush." He retracted all of his fingers and sat back down.

"I want to go home. Get me out of this place."

He reached for me and held me close to him. "Be patient a while longer. We cannot leave just yet. It wouldn't be polite."

We sat there for maybe half an hour more, then Gray stood up. "We can go now."

Outside a fog had come into the city. I pulled my jacket in close. "Jesus. What was that all about?"

He didn't say anything immediately, just looked around the street and acted like he was listening for something. "It went better than I expected. I think we can talk now. It was about the egg."

"Christ!" Gray can really be a pain in the ass sometimes. "I know that. Who was the Centaur? Why did we need to come here? Did he really destroy your nest—home or whatever? Talk to me!''

Gray seemed to mull over that for a minute or two. ''There is only one Centaur on earth. Even if there were more, this one is special. He is the—'Bishop' really is the best word, I think. I have met him slightly several times. His family and my family disputed over some territory in the Maxwell Station system. My family was destroyed, or if not completely destroyed forced to evacuate the system. I do not know where they are. Your parents found me in the asteroid belt about a thousand years later. I thought the egg might be a Centaur egg, but I could not find out directly—Centaurs do not allow much personal information about them to be published. They will talk about almost anything, but allow very little of it to be written down. All I was able to find out was that there was only one Centaur family on earth, and that it was the Bishop's.''

I shuddered. ''Would he really have eaten me?''

Gray nodded. ''They consider presentients a delicacy.''

''Presentients?''

''A Centaur has odd and rigid rules over what is a person and what is not: communication defines a person in most circumstances.''

''Jesus! I could have talked to him!''

''I know that.''

I hit him on the leg. ''Why did you tell me to keep it a secret? I could have been killed. It just seems stupid.''

97

We kept walking. "If you had spoken, he might have challenged you to an eating duel."

"I can eat with the best of them."

"An eating duel," said Gray carefully, "is a duel in which the loser gets eaten. To the Centaurs, losers are not persons by definition."

"Oh," I said, feeling very small. "Why was I here at all, then?" I felt so lost and confused.

"I did not want the Bishop to think I had come for revenge. If I brought my family, he would know for certain I had not come for war. I don't want to die either, Ira."

We walked a little further and I reached up and took his hand. "I'm sorry about your family, Gray."

Gray didn't say anything for a block or so. "They are gone."

As evening had fallen, a fog had come into town from the nooks and canals of Back Bay, rolled into the city like a stumbling drunk. As the elevator descended towards it, Sara had the feeling of diving into water or cotton or something else she could drown in. She was to meet Sam on his boat about eight. But right now, she needed a drink. She left the building almost as soon as she hit the ground floor.

Now, she was below the bright sunlight she had left on the ninetieth floor. The fog had given the city a dreamy, half-real quality. The locust trees in front of the old Customs House burned yellow through it, the fall colors pastel and washed out. The upper city was completely lost.

Here, there was only this corner, filled with tourist shops, street vendors, and a man selling flowers, each close and intimate in the fog.

She bought a pretzel from a cart and waited while the man warmed it in one of those battery-powered alien ovens. One of those would be good on the *Hercules,* she thought.

Sitting beneath the locust trees and eating slowly, guiltily—Sam would be cooking dinner for her in a couple of hours—she was suddenly struck with the memory of Hull, burning. For a long moment, she could smell the explosions like fireworks mixed with the smell of burning houses and the sea. She remembered hitting a nameless man across the face with a crowbar—dark Asian hair, stubble, wild eyes, blood spilling from his forehead as he fell into the water—when he had tried to take the whaler away from her. She had tried to get to the house—the only house she had ever known after a lifetime of living on boats, that her father and mother wouldn't leave and would not believe they had to leave until it was too late—when she found Roni, burned, arm broken, half swimming through the hip-deep water. Sara dragged Roni into the whaler. She started up the motor again to get to the house when the MDC planes came in low and dropped something—she never knew what—that exploded into a sheet of flame. The firestorm raced towards them in a boiling, guttering wave. She turned the whaler and gunned the motors. The flames leaped from house to house, low-pitched explosions following her. Don't foul the prop!

Don't foul the prop! The whaler burst out into the harbor. Up on Telegraph Hill, the gangs were shooting back. Hog Island was firing antiaircraft guns at the MDC planes. Two planes banked towards it, fired two missiles—Sara grabbed Roni and dove into the bottom of the boat. There was a blinding flash and the sea roared around them. A hot wind sucked the breath from her lungs. There was a sound too loud to be understood. Then, it passed and utter silence came to her. Am I deaf?

She looked back and Hog Island was flattened. The fires had been blown by the wind into smoke.

Sara sat unseeing on the park bench, holding herself. She could never even identify where her house had been, much less her parents. It had taken hours just to find the *Hercules*. At least, that was intact. There were no looters. Maybe they were dead. Maybe they had been blinded by the flash. Maybe Sara was so deep in shock she couldn't see them. She left Hull, the smoke masking the sun into a deep red disk hanging sickly in the west, a cold south wind blowing them towards Boston. Roni never took her eyes off Sara that whole night. She watched every move Sara made.

Sara looked up at the locust tree and shook herself. Almost seven. Time to go. She stood up slowly, shaking off the memory. Someday, someday, she would bury that memory. Roni getting herself killed only made it worse. "Damn you, Roni," she said under her breath. "I didn't drag you out of there just to die like a dog."

It was that same south wind that blew across her on the way home. She lit a cigarette and rummaged in the whaler's small hold. There was a half-empty fifth of rye whisky buried under a tow line. Do we want to begin here? Yes, I think we do. It is always better to begin early. You're in too lousy a mood for dinner with Jesus Christ himself, much less Sam. That's it. Take a good one. Feel that deep, aching warmth burn in your belly.

Jack was waiting for her on the *Hercules*.

"Hey, honey," she said as she tied up. "I'm home."

Jack nodded shortly. He leaned against the hull and stared moodily out the window.

Damn. He's acting like a teenager again. "Something wrong?"

"No."

"Sam asked me over to his boat for dinner." No response. "Your Mama's got a date."

Jack didn't look at her. "That's good," he said distractedly.

Damn. He's getting more like his father every day. Don't think about Mike. Don't. He was slime. He was scum. And didn't I want him back for the longest time?

She sat next to him and watched him in the darkening light. The whisky and the sunset light met and mellowed in her. Ah, Sara. Don't you miss him, though.

"Hey, honey," she said softly.

Jack looked at her, and she started to reach out and hold him but she could feel him stiffen. "What's the matter, Jack?"

Jack shrugged. "I don't know. I'm still thinking about it." He looked up at her searchingly, then seemed to find something that reassured him. He grinned. "I'll be okay. You go have a good time with Sam. Gonna find me a pop?"

It was an old joke, but thin now. She slapped his knee lightly. "Watch your mouth. Christ. I've got to take a shower."

She left Jack on the *Hercules* sometime later, walked nervously over to Sam's *Casey*. She was wearing a dress—she hadn't worn a dress in years. She was even wearing earrings.

Sam was wearing a jacket—from the way he wore it, he hadn't worn a jacket in years, either. That made her feel better.

He didn't say anything as he gestured her inside, then leaned down and whispered conspiratorially: "I've got steak."

"Go on." She laughed.

"No. Honest." He pointed to the galley. "It's in there. You can see it for yourself."

"That's a day's salary."

"Steak," he said. "Meat. Beef. *Carne. Le boeuf.* Thick, juicy, broiled, bloody—"

She laughed and touched his mouth to make him stop and he did and her fingertips tingled. Sara pulled them back and folded her arms, embarrassed.

"Anyway," he said suddenly after a silence,

"I've got it. And we're gonna eat it. You may as well adjust."

"I'm adjusted. Let's eat it now."

He shook his head and held up his hands, palms towards her. "Not so fast. We have to make preparations. We can't insult the cattle gods."

She sat down and began to laugh. It was uncontrollable and she sobbed and held her stomach.

"It wasn't that funny," he said with a shy grin.

"Damn you." She giggled. "You did this to me in high school, too. I'd forgotten."

"My dear, my dignity is ruined."

"Christ, it's good to see you again."

He didn't reply. "Dinner is served."

Steak was rare. Usually meat came like a slab, grown in the huge meat farms in the midwest. *Steak* came from an *animal*. A cow? No. Steer. It came from a steer. Steak was expensive.

Sam had broiled it perfectly.

"Do you like it?"

She nodded and made an incoherent noise around a piece of gristle.

Half an hour later, she leaned back and patted her full stomach. "I am satisfied. Life is good."

Sam leaned towards her. "There's more."

She shrugged. "It could only be a letdown."

He reached above them and out of a cabinet pulled down a bottle. "I don't think so." He handed her the bottle.

Her eyes grew round. "Glenfiddich! Christ on a stick! How long have you had this?"

Sam grinned at her and leaned on the table. "My daddy gave it to me. He brought it back from Scotland a few years ago."

"Christ," she said again. "This is too much. Put it back, Sam."

"Too late." He brought down two glasses. "You don't want me to drink alone."

The scotch made her feel warm and sleepy, like the world no longer had hard edges. Sam turned on the radio and they listened to some fluffy pop station. She didn't like it. "Turn it to something else." She took the bottle and held it lovingly in her arms. "Got a cigarette?" she said.

"Don't smoke."

"He doesn't smoke," she said to the bottle. "He's a wonder, Sam is."

Sam found a jazz station, faint but clear. "That's better." He hummed along with a clarinet.

"Yeah," she said and half filled both their glasses.

"Want to dance?" he said with a faint giggle.

"Sure."

They stood up and swayed together and he felt so right, in her arms, close, moving slowly together to the faint jazz. It had been so long, she wanted to cry. Just to be touched. Just to be warm with someone else.

Outside, she heard a cry.

"Jack?" she said and the scotch blew through her mind.

There was somebody shouting and somebody answering.

"Jack!" She was outside. Sam followed her but she didn't notice. Gray was standing outside the cabin holding Jack up in the air, struggling. The cabin inside was a mess, the cushions were slashed. The table was overturned.

"Let him go!" she shrieked, grabbed a crowbar. *"Let him go!"*

Ira launched himself at her and grabbed her arms. The gouge on the bar looped in the air towards his face. Gray's fingers closed on it and held it as if it were set in concrete.

There was a long minute where Gray held Jack in one set of arms, the crowbar in another, and grasped the railing with a third. "Jack is all right," he said and pulled the crowbar from her.

"Jesus," she heard Sam say behind her.

Jack stood absolutely still.

"What is going on?" she asked him. "What is going on?"

Jack looked at her, then at Ira, Gray, back at her. Back to Gray.

"What happened?" she asked Gray.

Gray did not speak for a long minute, watching Jack. "I do not know. I do not know what is happening at all."

"And what the hell happened to the goddamn cabin?" Sara demanded.

"I did it," said Gray slowly. "It was an accident. I did not mean to. I misjudged things. I will fix it. I will fix it sometime tomorrow."

"Tomorrow!" Ira burst out. "We were going . . .'' and his voice trailed off. He looked at Sara and then looked down.

"Going where?'' she said, suspicious. Where would Ira be going that he would hide it? "The ferry. You two were going to the *Hesperus* tomorrow?''

Gray nodded. "We were.''

She looked at him coldly. "I told you not to take him there.''

He did not speak.

"Don't do it again. I won't have you around if you do that. I won't have you anywhere near me.'' She stood up next to him and stared up into his face. She could feel the nearness of his rhino body, hear the rasp of leather as he breathed. "You hear me? You understand this time?''

He seemed to shrink on himself a little. "I understand.''

"Sara,'' softly from behind her. "It's not that big a thing.''

Sara whirled on Sam. "Get off my boat, Sam. Don't tell me how to raise my family. Get out of here.''

Sam shook his head as if he'd been slapped. He stiffly turned and walked back towards his own boat.

"Okay,'' she said. "Okay now.'' She turned to Jack and Ira. "Get inside and into bed. That's enough. There aren't going to be any more fireworks tonight.''

I was lying in the bunk an arm's length from Jack. I could hear him breathing, snuffling sometimes, and muttering. Damn. I don't know what he was doing when we came back, but it was him, not Gray, that had ripped up the cabin. Him. And Gray'd lied for him. Gray would never lie for me.

Gray'd never lied before.

Before, that I knew about, I said to myself. How'd I know what was lie and what was truth?

All my life, I'd been with Gray and now it was like something had been pulled out from under me. He wasn't mine anymore. I leaned over on my side and shook my head.

"Ira?" said Jack softly.

"What do you want?"

He didn't say anything for a minute. "I'm sorry I called Gray names."

Sorry. Yeah, right. Gray liked the son of a bitch. Gray *protected* him. Christ.

"Ira?"

"I heard you."

There was a rustle in the cabin and I knew he was turned towards me. "I've been pretty mean to you."

I didn't say anything.

He leaned back and made some kind of a sound, like crying maybe. Like coughing. "I'm sorry."

Like that made it better or something.

"You know," he said.

I just wished he'd shut up. I didn't want to hear him.

"You know," he said again. "I never knew

my dad. He split before I was born. And with Mama the way she is, we never really had a family. Now, with you and Gray—it's as if I had a real family."

I sat up and looked at him. "I ain't your brother. Gray can be if he wants to. I don't want any part of you." I stood up. He didn't move, just watched me. "I don't want any part of your friggin' mother. Or you. Or Gray. I just want to get shut of the whole friggin' lot of you." I finished getting dressed. "If the whole mess of you died, I'd piss on your grave."

I left, quiet like, so nobody'd be awakened. I looked outside, but Gray was gone. Good riddance. I was on my own now. It was just me.

I walked through the marshes towards the egg. Day was just coming around. The light was kind of a pale violet. I stopped in the marsh and watched it. My Mama stood with it and watched it with me.

"You're misjudging Gray," she said.

I looked at her. "I don't want you telling me what to judge and not. You're dead." I turned back towards the wreck and didn't wait to see if she disappeared or not.

The ferry was the same. Sunlight was just pouring over the hull when I got there, golden and rosy. The egg was where we'd left it—where I'd left it. It was bigger yet. The skin seemed swelled almost to bursting.

"You and me," I said to it. And it seemed like it could hear me. "You and me. We'll take a ride around the world. I don't care if you're a griffin or a dragon or anything.'' Tears started to leak out of my eyes. I shook them away. ''I don't care. We'll get out of this goddamn place. You and me.''

The egg didn't say anything and the tears started up again.

Sara got up too and sat in the head for a while. It had been a while since she had drunk that much. Her head felt hot and she rested it against the hatch to cool it. After a little while, she felt better. She went out into the main cabin, but didn't want to go back to bed. The cold and lonely bed frightened her for some reason.

Mike. I still want you to come back.

The thought came to her out of the clear darkness in the back of her mind. Fourteen years and she hadn't left it behind.

She sat in one of the chairs in the galley and lit a cigarette. And Sam—did he know what he was getting into? What a snake pit. She wished she hadn't snapped at him. He was only trying to be a good guy.

Yeah. Right. She inhaled the cigarette savagely. Good guys. They're all good guys. Sam was no different.

''Mama?'' came from behind her.

She turned. It was Jack, half dressed and looking at her vaguely. Had Mike looked that young when they were in school? ''Yeah, honey?''

''It wasn't Gray who ripped up the cushions.''

He stood next to her and watched, his eyes dry and calm. As if he'd already cried until he had cried himself out but still had one thing left to do.

"Who did it, honey?"

"I did. Gray and Ira came back and I went crazy, ripping the place apart. I just went crazy."

She pulled him to her and held him. He submitted to it, leaning against her. So this is what it's come to, Roni. I got to get rid of them. Gray for sure. Maybe Ira, too. Because, Roni, in the end, at the final curtain, nothing means as much to me as my little boy. Not you. Not Ira— certainly not Gray. Not Sam. Not even Mike, gone for so long. In the end, it's me and him.

"It's all right, honey." She held him tight. I'm sorry, Roni. That's the way it is. "It's all right."

After a while, he pulled away and looked at her sideways, then turned and shuffled back to bed. He closed the door after him.

She stayed up and smoked another cigarette, thinking how to tell Gray. He was first. He would have to leave tomorrow. Then. Then, we would see about Ira.

She must have sat there for at least an hour, thinking, dreaming. The sky began to lighten and the sun rose.

There was an eruption of water outside and the entire boat shook as Gray landed on the deck. Dripping he stalked into the cabin, ran past Sara, and ripped the door open.

"Jack! Where is Ira?"

Sara stood and saw past Gray Ira's empty bed. "Oh, my God."

Jack looked up at Gray. "I don't know. He left a couple of hours ago."

Sara cried out. "Why didn't you tell me, Jack?"

Jack looked at her out of Mike's blue eyes—different now, colder, stronger. "He wanted to go and he didn't want me along. I wanted to protect him. Like Gray protected me."

"Loyal child," said Gray. "But foolish. No. I am the fool." He turned and began to leave the cabin.

"Gray, wait!"

"No time! The boy is in danger. I did not follow him, thinking he was too upset. It was time for him to be by himself. But he disappeared like a ghost to me. He is gone."

"Where are you going?" she wailed after him.

"The wreck. The egg is hatching—I fear it."

"Wait—damn you, wait! We can take the whaler. It's got a good motor. It'll get us there quicker than you can go."

He stopped for a moment, absolutely still. Looked down at her. "You are right. I will take it."

"You will not! It's mine, like Jack's my kid and Ira's my nephew."

Gray shook his head. "You are right. I will follow."

They climbed into the whaler and thank God it started the first time for once. Gray sat in the middle and they left the dock and shot out across the harbor at full speed.

"What is this egg, anyway?" she yelled above the wind.

"I don't know. We found it in the wreck and it pleased the boy to hatch it. I thought it no danger—at first I thought it might be a Centaur egg."

Sara felt befuddled. Centaurs? "A Centaur?"

"A species that would consider Ira a delicacy." He held his hands together and even in that position Sara could sense the anguish in him. "But I asked the Bishop and the Bishop said there were no eggs here. So I felt safe. No other egg species here is dangerous."

"So there's no danger."

"There is always danger, but I thought I could head it off and still let the boy play for a while. But now the thing hatches and Ira is away from me. I do not know what the thing is." He fell silent. "His mother and father might protect him."

"What?"

He turned to her. "He sees his mother and father at times. They speak to him. They may lead him away."

"Are you crazy?"

"No."

"Ira sees ghosts? Christ. The poor kid. Making this up."

The wind cut through them and the spray splattered across them as Sara turned the boat inland. They could already see the *Hesperus* outlined dark against the beach and the rising sun.

"I am not sure he is making them up."

112

"You've been encouraging this? I don't believe it. They aren't real." She wished she had a cigarette. That's it. Gray had to go.

Gray looked at her out of those huge eyes.

"How do you know they aren't?"

For her life, she could not answer.

The egg was moving a little now. Kind of wobbling side to side.

I looked and found this old metal bar to help break the egg, help the dragon get loose. I stood next to it—it was smelling pretty ripe now—and didn't do anything. I couldn't decide. Even dragons might be fragile when they were still in the egg. I could hurt it. I chewed on my lip and put down the bar, sat back, and watched it.

"Ira? Ira!" called my father from the edge of the boat. I wasn't going to go see them. They were just ghosts. They called again. Oh, well. The egg was going to be a little longer, I figured. I went to the edge and looked down. Both of them were there.

"Come down here," called Papa. Mama nodded. "Come down," she said.

I sat on the edge of the hull and shook my head. "I don't want to listen to you anymore. You're dead. Gray's gone weird on me. I don't like Aunt Sara and Jack. Leave me alone. I got my egg."

They looked at one another.

"Son?" said my father softly. "Gray and Sara are coming to get you. They'll take you back. You know they will."

113

I could hear a motor on the other side of the wreck. "Are you trying to fool me?"

Papa shook his head. "Absolutely not. They're almost here."

"What about the egg?"

"The egg can take care of itself. Come on!" yelled my mother.

I jumped the three meters down to the beach and tumbled. It hurt my feet.

Mama and Papa lead me into the marsh. Deep into the swamp, hurrying me, urging me to go so fast I couldn't see where I was going. I could barely breathe for running. The tall grass whipped my face and the mud was knee-deep. Where the hell was I? Finally, they stopped.

I sat down in the water. I couldn't breathe. Nothing in the world was so important as breathing.

"He's safe now," said Mama.

"What?" I said and looked up. They were gone. They were gone and I didn't know where the hell I was. They'd tricked me. "Goddamn you!" I yelled after them. "Goddamn you to hell!"

Gray moved to the front of the boat, looking for all the world like a hound ready to leap in the water after fallen birds.

"Back a little, for Christ's sake," yelled Sara. "Don't swamp the boat."

"I can't find him."

"Of course you can't find him. We're not there yet."

"You don't understand. Since I knew them, I have always known where they were. Ira is all that is left. Now he is gone." Gray turned towards Sara. "He is no longer a child. Perhaps that is why I cannot find him."

Sara shrugged. When this was over, Gray had to leave before he made her crazy. "That egg's in the wreck, right?"

"Yes."

"Then that's where he'll be."

They beached the whaler and moved around the side of the wrecked ferry.

"Where is the egg?"

"In the center of the wreck."

Sara looked at the rusty hull. "We're going to have to climb that?"

Gray shook his head. "There is no time," he said. He picked her up and held her in two sets of arms, then leaped to the top of the hull. He released her and moved purposefully inward. She followed.

In the center of the wreck, the sunlight had already made the area warm. The egg was moving.

"Ira?" called Gray. Sara called also.

"That thing's going to hatch soon." The thing was huge now, almost a meter broad and the surface was a writhing pink and green.

"He is not here." Gray turned towards her. "We had best back away from it."

The egg exploded. A shard caught Sara's shoulder and knocked her down. Something brightly colored that seemed to be made chiefly

115

of mouth and teeth and tail shot into the air and hovered over them. It moved jerkily, its huge, outsized mouth opening and closing mechanically. It quivered. Shook itself in the air. Pawed at its teeth, pulling shards of broken eggshell out from between its fangs. Sara watched it, frozen. Unable to move so much as her eyeballs from the thing. It was a dragon. Its feathers were a golden orange, its eyes a brilliant green. Its wings beat too fast to be seen—but she could feel the air from them. It looked around, cocked its head this way and that as if testing the air. Then it saw her.

It seemed to smile. And Sara wanted to scream but she had not time. As suddenly as it saw her it dove—faster than anything she had ever seen, faster than anything had a right to be. Something huge and massive and equally fast shot over her and intercepted the dragon.

The dragon screamed, and its talons and teeth were a blur. Gray made a noise like a cry and tried to knock it away, and it rolled away in the air, tumbling and screaming. It caught itself and shot above them, saw Gray, and dove for him. Gray was ready this time and there was a brief blur of movement—each slashing, the dragon biting—that seemed to take forever. Then the dragon tumbled across the deck and slammed the hull so hard it rang. It shook its head and moaned. Gray leaped over to it, all over knives now. Each arm sprouted a dozen. He slashed it, and the dragon screamed and tore off one of his arms. Gray picked it up with another arm and slammed it again the hull. The dragon tried to reach the hand holding it but couldn't. Gray slammed it against the hull again. He slammed it again. It sounded like a pile driver. The dragon clawed at him but had no strength. He slammed it again and again until it no longer moved and then he continued, methodically and mechanically.

Sara approached him. The dragon was a bloody mess. "Gray?"

Gray did not answer but slammed the dragon into the wall.

"Gray? I think it's dead."

Gray looked at her, then at the dragon. "Oh." Then he looked at himself. "Oh." He sat back and stared at the stump of his arm. "I am hurt." There were slashes through the armor on his chest and arms. The hand at the end of one of his other arms was nearly chewed off. All of the wounds oozed something like tar.

"What can I *do*, Gray?"

"Do? Oh. Yes." He looked over to where the egg had been. "One of those old mattresses. And the tarp."

She dragged the mattress to him, and he tore out the padding and stuffed it in the slashes and the stump of his arm. The oozing stopped.

He looked at her. "I will live. I have repair cement at home to cover this, then I will be better."

Sara sat back and shook her head, laughed tensely, softly. Of course. "Repair cement."

117

He looked at her. "Spatiens do not heal. They must be repaired."

"You sound like you think you're a robot."

"No." He appeared thoughtful. "Not exactly. Spatiens were built thousands of years ago. Those that did this are dead or gone now. We are all that's left." He looked at her. "Think of me as an archaeological find that has been somewhat damaged."

She laughed again. He moved and she saw the dragon, all needles and teeth. "What was it?"

"An object of my stupidity." He balled one fist and for a moment, Sara thought he was going to hit it again. Instead, he pushed the bedding tighter into his wounds. "Stupid. I thought only the Centaurs could be creatures such as this. All things like to share their heritage. This is one of the Centaurs' pets."

"A pet. Dear God. A pet." She pulled her knees up to her chin and felt very cold.

Gray looked up. "That tarp. Get me that tarp. He's coming back."

She brought the tarp to him, and he wrapped it around his body into a sort of toga. "What are you doing?"

"It is shameful to show wounds that have not been cared for. At least, it is shameful to show them to your children."

She looked at him. "Children?"

"You did not know? You are all, all of you, my family. Why else would I follow him here? Why would I try so hard to understand you? Why

118

would I spend my life for you? To me, what else could you be?''

I ran back toward the wreck. My side felt like somebody'd taken and shoved a hot poker in it. My face felt hot like I was going to cry. Tricked. By my own folks. By my own parents. I sat down next to a clump of Indian rice and cried and rested until I could breathe again. Christ. *Christ!*

I saw it fly above the wreck, catch the sun, flying so fast I could barely see it. Like a hummingbird, maybe. Like a dragon. It flew back down into the ferry and I couldn't see it anymore.

After a minute or two, I could move and walked back to the ferry. It was quiet. I climbed up on the hull and sneaked around to the center to see if the egg was all right.

It was like one of those pictures you see in magazines, distant, not meaning anything until you see one little feature that hits you like a fist.

They were sitting next to the hull, just watching me. The egg was all broken up. Gray was all tangled up in a tarp. The dragon—and it had been a dragon, after all—was all crumpled up next to the wall.

I stepped towards them. They were just watching me. Gray wrapped up like that reminded me of when they brought Papa home, all bandaged up and covered with blood, the miners singing that mournful song. I'd never heard anybody but Papa sing that song before, and I couldn't forget it now. It just ran over and over in my head:

I dreamed I saw Joe Hill last night,
alive as you and me.
I said, "Joe Hill you're ten years dead."
"I never died," said he.

And they couldn't find Mama, just pieces of her 'cause the supervisors had thrown a grenade and she'd caught it and it had blown up before she could throw it away. Papa's face was so still. And I knew he was dead, gone, and everything I ever wanted from him seemed small, and I seemed small. Damn you, I wanted to say then. Damn you for leaving me. I never wanted that. Fuck the miners. Fuck the supervisors.

And the dragon was dead. My ticket away. And Gray was standing there, shrouded like he was dead. "Fuck you! Goddamn you, Gray! Goddamn you, Sara! Fuck you! Fuck this boat! Fuck the dragon! *Fuck all of you!*"

I just stood there, swearing, and I wanted to pick up things and throw them at them the way I wanted to hurt the miners that brought Papa home, the way I wanted to hurt him for leaving me.

I felt strangled, dying. I stared at them, quiet now. They didn't say anything. I left the ferry and went back into the marsh and collapsed. I beat the ground with my fists and my feet. It wasn't fair. Everybody left me. Everybody ran away and I was just left there, alone.

"Jesus," Sara said at last, and started to follow Ira.

"Wait." Gray touched her gently and his voice sounded more weary and defeated than any voice she had ever heard. "He needs—to be alone, perhaps." Gray pushed himself to his feet and part of the tarp fell from him. He tried clumsily to cover himself. The rents in his skin made her feel queasy. He swayed on his feet. "I am no fit member of your family. All things I have tried to do I have failed. I—"

"Hush," she said and tried to steady him. "Let's go home. Ira will come home eventually."

"I do not know what to do." Gray breathed softly. She could smell him this close, and he smelled rich and strong, like sweat or bread. She helped him to the ocean side of the ferry, and he climbed down as slowly and as carefully as an old man.

He did not move in the boat until she got him home. He stumbled as he walked next to her onto the dock and into the boat. Jack was there and helped her put him in her bed.

"Where's the repair cement?" she asked.

Gray looked at her as if from a great distance. "In the equipment locker. Next to the diesel starter fluid."

Sara found a can with various symbols she could not read hidden behind a can of oil. It belonged in the medicine cabinet, she decided. Enough of this separateness.

Jack didn't say a word, and the two of them cleaned the tattered tarp and bedding out of the wounds and filled them with cement using a putty knife. Gray gave them soft instructions, but after a time his voice fell silent and Sara thought him asleep. She motioned Jack out of the cabin and began to leave herself.

"Thank you," said Gray suddenly.

She turned to him and realized he no longer looked alien to her. Different, yes. But he looked the way she would have expected him to look. Scarred. Tired. He belonged there.

"It's a small thing to do for someone who saved my life." She shrugged and looked out the porthole to the bow. He'd been sleeping there all summer. "We need to build you a real room. There's not enough room for you here."

"I do not need much."

She smiled at him. "None of us do. But nobody in my family sleeps in the open like an animal."

Sara thought she heard a second thank you behind her, but she wasn't sure. It wouldn't have mattered if she had.

Jack was looking at her anxiously. "Is he going to be all right?"

"I don't know." Sara looked back toward the cabin. "I hope so."

Jack looked at her, then down at the ground, then back at her. "Are you going to send him away?"

Sara sat at the table in the galley. She lit a cigarette and wished she had a drink. "Do you want me to?"

Jack shook his head.

She exhaled smoke. "Okay. How come?"

" 'Cause—" He stopped, embarrassed. "He deserves to be here."

"I agree. I'm not going to send him away."

Jack looked relieved. "I was scared you would. On account of me." His eyes grew wide. "Where's Ira?"

"Out. He'll be back soon." I hope.

She could tell from Jack's face he didn't believe her. Well, she'd never been able to tell a lie to Mike, either. But Jack wasn't his father. Christ. It was stupid to even think that way. Mike's been gone fourteen years, for God's sake.

Sara reached over and gripped him by the shoulder for a minute, and he came over to her and they sat there holding each other for some minutes.

She heard Ira before she saw him. He came in, sullen, wildness in his eyes. Christ, he looked like Roni. How come she'd never seen it? And he was such a *little* kid, barely even there.

"Go on, Jack," she said softly. "Go on over to Kendall's. Stay there tonight."

Jack looked first at her, then at Ira, then nodded to himself and left.

The silence lay between Ira and Sara for some minutes.

"I came by to get my things," he said.

"Oh?" She inhaled and tried to think. What could she do? What the hell was going on in that small head?

"Yeah. I'm leaving. I ain't got no place here."

His eyes were just like Roni's. Stubborn, too. Just as stubborn as she was when she left.

She stubbed her cigarette out. "Look. I want you here. You're my nephew. You're my blood. I want Gray here. Christ. But I'm not keeping anybody here who doesn't want to stay." His expression didn't change. I guess I wouldn't be convinced, either, she thought. She tried to be cool. "Your stuff's in your room. Gray's in my room, resting. You ought to say good-bye to him."

Ira snorted. "I don't want to. I'm getting out of here."

Something snapped in Sara. She grabbed Ira and pushed him down in the chair. "You little shit. What the hell do you think you're doing? Gray went out there to save your little ass."

"Gray killed my dragon. I wanted to get out of here."

"That thing was going to have you for lunch! Gray saved me. He saved you. And he was damned near killed doing it. You want to leave? Fine. You do it. You take your things and get the hell out. Somebody saves your life and you don't give a damn? Fine. You take your ungrateful, snot-nosed face out of here. But you will thank him before you leave or I'll beat you black and blue. You got that? You hear me?"

He stared at her.

She sat back in the chair, ashamed. Aren't things bad enough without your shouting at a little boy? Tact. That's what you got in spades, Sara. "He's in there."

Ira stood up hesitantly, looked at the door to

the cabin, then back at her. He touched the door, looked inside, entered the room.

She heard faint voices, harsh sounds, then a gentle quiet. Suddenly, she felt like everything would be all right. That and a warmth and a strength she hadn't felt for years. It was like a kind of singing inside her. She stepped outside and smelled the October sea air. It was brisk.

Gray and Ira didn't need her right then.

She walked down to Sam's boat and knocked on the railing. After a few minutes, Sam looked out.

"Hi," he said warily.

"Hello, there," she said cheerfully. "Want to dance?"

"Gray?" I said softly. "Are you here?"

"In front of you," he said. I'd never heard him tired before.

"Are you okay?"

He didn't say anything for a minute. "No."

I turned on the light. His chest was all over covered with that repair gunk, big deep gashes. Oh, God. And he looked so tired and shrunken, like his skin didn't fit him anymore. "Oh, Gray."

He reached out and drew me to his side, and I started crying. He held me and I'd never felt so small and helpless, like I was a baby or broken or dead. "I never meant it, Gray. I never meant it. Don't go away." Mama had gone away and Papa had gone away and if Gray went away too there'd be nobody.

"Hush," he said in a croon. "Hush, Ira. I'm not going anywhere. I love you. Sara loves you. Nobody's leaving anybody."

I thought I heard Mama and Papa near me but I didn't look for them. I didn't need to.

Gray slowly grew warm and soft and he held me. He almost filled the bed and I had to scrunch up against the hull, but I didn't mind. After a while he looked down at me.

"What are the three loves?"

"Jerk." I hit him very softly on one of his good arms. "I'll never forget. Love of family, love of work, and love of duty." I sat up and looked at him right in those big eyes of his. "And always, *always*, in that order."

Maxwell Station: 2027 AD

Gilbert Bloom stood looking out a window.

He hated it.

The window was framed in cherry with oak veneer. There was a pink and white lace curtain moving in a faint breeze. The panes were old, the glass had flowed downstream, and the view was distorted.

The window looked out into space. In the distance, improbably large, were the other four planets of the Pauli system. Insystem from the viewer was a gaudy ring around the sun. Then, below them, turned a yellow and red world— Maxwell Station, thought Gilbert, tasting the words, wanting to go there. That's where I should be. Between them and the Station turned two doughnuts speared by a pencil: the orbital plat-form, *Proud Mary*.

That's where I should be. I should be working.

You got to work. You got to build something.

He leaned his head through the image of the window and felt the cold steel of the walls. The rest of the apartment was gray steel. A good gray, he thought. An honest gray. Like real work. Not a lie like the window graphic.

He heard Roni rustle in the apartment's other room, a soft tone from the display unit.

Another letter? Christ! She wrote Sara last week! People bleeding to death must feel this way. A hemorrhage here, a drop there, each little bit a draw on capital. Work. He had to find work.

And this damned window! Artificial as hell, looking down on the place where he lived, hang-ing over a place he would probably never see.

"Damnit, Roni! How often do you have to write her, anyway." He pushed away from the wall—the window never even rippled—and walked into the other room.

"It's just a letter."

"It's money. Everything takes money. Espe-cially things you send home to earth."

Roni glared at him. "Then, I'll *pay* for it."

At least, *she* had a job.

Hell, she hasn't even started yet.

But she's got one. Why can't you find a job?

"There aren't any here," he muttered.

"Aren't any what?"

"Nothing!" he said fiercely and stalked back into the bedroom and looked around. Get out of here. Go on down to the posting board. Yeah. Maybe they've got something there.

He started changing his clothes. "I'm going down to the government deck. Check the posting board."

"Did you check the net?"

"Of course I did. I'm unemployed, not stupid."

He found a tie and faced the mirror. Knot a tie around your neck like a noose. You have to look good. There could be something down there. When's the last real job you had? A year ago? Christ, I hate this place. Damn this ship to hell. Damn the bureaucrats that won't open goddamn Maxwell Station. Damn me for ever coming here.

"I didn't say you were stupid."

There's got to be something. The *Proud Mary*'s five kilometers long. Each of the doughnuts a kilometer across and three hundred meters thick. Who cares if the place is a ghost ship?

"What did you say?" He stared into the mirror. There's got to be something. Painting. Rewiring. Cooking, for God's sake. Something.

Gilbert walked back into their combination living room, study, dining room, and kitchen— the "other" room.

Roni smiled at him and for a moment he remembered why he married her: that smile got to him again. He smiled at her in return.

"I said"—she spoke softly—"that I didn't say you were stupid.

He put on a grin. "I'm going to get me a job."

She nodded. "Good luck. I'll be on my first shift when you get back."

His grin fell. There wasn't a job down there. He knew it. She knew it. It made him crazy, not working. Just made him crazy. Thinking of her working and not him made him crazy. Thinking of their son, Ira, frozen like a mackerel down in the sleeper tanks made him crazy. He had to get a job. There were no other options and not much more money.

"I'll be back later," he said.

"Gilbert—" he heard her say as he closed the door.

You go crazy without working, he thought. You just go crazy.

Roni pulled her hand back as he left. He didn't talk to her much anymore. She returned to her letter.

. . . I envy the people who took the sleep. Their costs are already paid for. Of course, if they are never needed, they will be shipped back and lose all that money. And that seems to be more and more likely. The cost of waiting is eating into our savings. Not taking the big sleep sure seemed a good idea at the time. I guess that is the way of all good intentions. At least, little Ira is safely sleeping. I miss him so much.

What's going on at home? Why are they taking so long? If you hear something, write us. The only news we get here is the official

IPOB announcements and you know what they're like. "Lengthy negotiations make determining the exact moment Maxwell Station will be open impossible." I ask you, is that English?

Write us anyway. How's Jack? Did Mike ever send the child support for him? How's the building trade in Boston? We heard from Sam recently. He dropped us a note from Shanghai. What was he doing there? It's a long way away from Hull.

That was a good stopping place. She signed her name, thought for a moment and erased it, then printed her name and Gilbert's, together, and pressed the Send button. The display flashed SENT in small, blinking letters and then faded.

For a moment, she wished she could see Sara, touch her. It was hard to imagine ever seeing her again. Even if things went right, they made a good stake, and returned home, Roni already felt so different here. A year and a half. Sara seemed more of a memory than a real person, a kind of half ghost.

Anything would seem a ghost if all you ever saw were gray steel walls. She could watch the window, anyway.

"Damn you, Gilbert," she muttered. At least we could spring enough credit to get a decent wall display.

She scratched her head—her newly short hair itched. Hydroworks had had her cut her hair. And paid for the medical work—both required for the job. She was to be the control, they had told her. She scratched her head again. When she was a child, she had looked in the mirror to see the spiral pattern of her hair on her head. She wondered what it looked like now. She wondered about Ira. Thank God, Ira is asleep. She hated feeling poor, hated even the thought that Ira would have to be here, watching them, feeling poor with them, watching them snap at each other—

Stop it.

God, she missed him.

She checked the time on the display. Just as well she stopped. It was time to go on shift. The only requirement of the hydroworks job was that she be punctual. That went double on the first day of the job.

The corridor outside toady was white—Roni guessed that whoever decided the graphic background hadn't made up his mind yet. Then, she looked closer. There was a billowing to the whiteness. A pair of white wolves suddenly ran towards her—she gasped and then they were behind her. The male looked back at her and grinned, lifted up his head, and howled soundlessly.

A blizzard. Cold. Cold and white.

She hurried down the corridor and took the lift down into the pencil. The corridor and the lift were empty.

Main Street, through the heart of the pencil, seemed crowded but it was a lie. On either side of her, the graphics on the wall were of people doing things: building bridges, drilling oil, fishing—all with either the name of Venture Capital or the discrete logo of Exterior Developments. One or the other owned the *Proud Mary*, but Roni didn't know which. All of the generic worker's faces glowed with satisfaction. But Main Street was eerily silent. She was surrounded by spirits.

At last, she came to Second Avenue. Across a giant double door, white like the hospital doors, was written HYDROWORKS.

The doors opened and a physician with a badge that said "Physician WHITE" stood and smiled at her.

"Come on in," said Physician White. "We've been expecting you."

Roni hated the smells automatically. Hospital smells. After Hull, Roni and Sara had searched the morgues for their parents. Morgues always smelled like hospitals, or they were in hospitals. She hated both places.

Physician White frowned at her. "You *are* here about the job, aren't you?"

"Yeah," said Roni at last. "I'm here about the job. I talked to somebody across the net. He said it was unskilled contracting that paid well."

" 'The least skill for the most pay,' I believe the ad said." Physician White led her inside, down a hall, and into a small room. "You did have the medical work done? And you read the pamphlet?"

Roni nodded. "Two venous shunts. Sick bay did them last week—you should know. They sent the results to you. And I read the pamphlet: 'Hazard Work and You.' Now I know everything. It's a living, I suppose."

Inside the small room was a large padded chair. Tubes came down from the ceiling and hung next to the chair—Roni suddenly knew where the venous shunts were going to connect. Wires sprouted like Medusa's hair from the headrest. She remembered Gilbert's parents' rose trellis in Dorchester.

Physician White strapped her into the chair and began to read from a piece of paper.

"Mrs. Bloom. You are to nod or otherwise give assent at this time that you know the following: 'the homeostasis of the *Proud Mary* is based on a Targive modified living system that is generally designed for any living organism within certain limits. The homeostatic system requires a control—you are to be that control for the duration of this shift, for the next eight hours.' Do you understand the above?"

"I read that in the pamphlet."

"Good." He began reading again.

" 'You are being engaged as a contractor and hereby agree to perform certain work, knowledge of which has been provided to you in the form of the booklet, "Hazard Work and You," a copy of which has been provided you, and agree to undergo certain precautionary and enhancement procedures in accordance with the work. You understand that the precautions are furnished without implied warranty and that the company assumes no liability for errors, omissions, or defects which may occur during the pendancy of the contract, including and without limitation, discomfort, disfigurement, pain, injury, permanent loss of facilities, or death. . . .' "

Roni had heard a similar litany at the beginning of every odd job for which she had scrambled in the last year and a half. Her mind wandered. Every person on the *Proud Mary* that wasn't crew had to work as a contractor. They'd work that way on Maxwell Station as well. That was the deal. Nobody expected Exterior Developments to take care of you.

"Do you understand this?"

She nodded mechanically.

Physician White coughed gently. "You have to actually say something out loud here."

"I agree. Can we get on with it?"

"Of course. Did the pamphlet tell you what to expect when the life support system is engaged?"

Roni closed her eyes and tried to remember. "It said there might be disorientation afterwards. That was all."

"Good. I didn't want you to experience anything you didn't expect." He nodded to someone behind Roni's chair. Two clicks of switches—

A dream:

A kind of violet hum passes through her and she is brought gently out of her body as easily as a letter is pulled from the envelope. What message is she? Whose words?

She flows through the Proud Mary, *water*

*through the veins, arteries, and brain down
through the walls; and for a moment, a long moment, she partakes of every person on the ship—
the physician watching over the meters, Gilbert
in front of the posting board, the thoughts of a
shuttle pilot as he pilots a starship into the dock
of the pencil—she must remember to tell Gilbert
about this. There might be work. Skald worrying
at the cost of making the planetfall amortized
over the year they have been waiting, up the
spokes to her quarters, looking down from the
ceiling, watching the spiral pattern growth of her
hair, she looks down on herself.*

*But this is not where she belongs. She floats
down through the deck and down into the sleeper
bins, hovering over his frozen face, taut and cold,
listening to the slow, slow electricity of her son's
thoughts as he waits for her, frozen. She cries
out for him and he answers her.*

Gilbert stood in front of the posting board, a
glass panel four meters long and a meter high,
with the postings printed on paper inside it. It
seemed everything dealing with the government
had to be done in the past.

Somebody had taped one of the original posted
advertisements for Maxwell Station on the glass:

OPPORTUNITIES!

Skilled and unskilled personnel are required
for dangerous and lucrative work in the building
of Maxwell Station.

Apply:
United States Civil Service
Department of Extraterrestrial Affairs
Division M

He remembered sitting in their small Quincey apartment, out on the point, Ira in his lap, watching the Boston arcology hazy in the distance, the single mile-high IPOB spire standing improbably black in the sunlight. They'd been able to see it from their kitchen table. He was thinking about Ira's future, their own, and how fascinated Ira had been when he had shown him the IPOB spire through the binoculars. There were aliens out there.

"Let's do it," he'd said.

You always remember where you were when you heard about them, like assassinations, disasters, and other great events.

Where were you when the aliens came?

2014: in the middle of a depression and financial collapse, an alien ship stopped in at Boston to get directions. Or as a religious pilgrimage. Or as economic envoys. Ask one person, you get one answer. Ask fifty and you get a hundred.

Maybe one of them is true. Maybe all of them.

They came with an economic interest in trade, an interesting set of laws and regulations, and the Loophole that joined earth to a kind of community of worlds.

Gilbert had been fifteen, looking up from his

backyard in Southie, watching the great gray *something* float in from the east, over the water, a long umbilical floating down touching the water.

They chose Boston as the point of entry. Washington and Moscow couldn't change their mind with force. Zurich couldn't change it with money. Rome couldn't change it with prayer. The Interstellar Port of Boston was chartered that same year.

Young Gilbert had wanted to dance. Later, he heard there was a parade through the heart of Boston, dancing and crying and laughing. He felt a deep bitterness that he'd missed it; that bitterness would stay with him for the rest of his life.

As Gilbert felt, so felt the rest of the country. Why should *we* be left out? Wasn't there enough to go around? Boston's great trading families helped: the Nyos, Mudandes, and Endicotts. They were the Bank. They were the Vault. They *were* Boston.

Venture Capital, the company that managed the local Loophole, found a planet that could be leased from its owners. Who those owners were was something of a mystery. Nyo Expeditions built the *Proud Mary*, and a collection of industrialists from Chicago, Los Angeles, and Pittsburgh formed Exterior Developments.

Twelve years after the aliens came, Gilbert had been working as a technical welder on the new Boston post office, one of the composite buildings in downtown Boston, and he'd mailed a letter.

Opportunities! said the sign.

"Let's do it," Gilbert at twenty-seven had said, and Gilbert at fifteen had cried out *yes*! Ira had leaned against his chest and fallen asleep. Ira's hair was blond still. It probably wouldn't darken until he was older. Gilbert's hadn't. His son reminded Gilbert of his father, his uncle, and stories his mother had told him about himself. *Why should we be left out?*

There had been thousands of little details. What to do about Roni's share in the family boat? It'd never mattered until now—Sara was living on it. But now, they might not come back at all. They might settle on Maxwell Station. Regardless, they would need the money from Roni's share as a stake. What to do about Ira? Take him? Couldn't keep him in the station with them—he couldn't pay his way. Leave him with Sara? But Roni was Ira's mother, not Sara, and Sara looked like she was going to have her hands full raising Jack. Mike had already left her at that point. They'd compromised—everything was a compromise—and paid for Ira to sleep until they could afford to wake him.

"Let's do it," he'd said after they'd figured out everything. They hadn't signed the papers, yet. Ira was sleeping against his chest, snoring softly. He had a son and a wife and he wanted to build an inheritance.

"Let's go out."

And now he was watching the goddamned posting board for a job. Now, when he should be working on Maxwell Station, mining antibiotics or processing biologicals or building the main buildings—or fifty other things.

The sign still read: OPPORTUNITIES!

He grabbed the notice and ripped it to pieces and threw it on the floor. *Screw* the posting board. *Screw* Maxwell Station.

He stopped: under the posting was a second posting, one asking for those with space suit experience.

REPORT TO GNOZA, XT DECK.

Gilbert grabbed the posting and ran.

Gnoza's office was listed as one of the general purpose cubbies in the heart of the special environments section—extraterrestrial deck. Gilbert let himself in.

Sitting at the desk, feet up on the edge, insolently sipping a beer was a small, incredibly wrinkled alien with huge blue eyes and an impossibly wide mouth.

"Gnoza?" asked Gilbert hesitantly.

"Right here. Sit down. I've been waiting for you." He reached into a fold of skin and brought out a cigar and lit it. Gilbert looked away, nauseated. He coughed politely. Gnoza ignored him.

"That smells horrible," said Gilbert through clenched teeth.

"Tough. You want a job?"

"Not enough to work around that." Wait! How bad did you want a job? He started to take it back but Gnoza grinned at him.

"Candy ass." Gnoza chuckled, but put out the cigar. "I got a job for you. I'm looking in the ring for an item to be named later. I need a man that knows his way around in a suit."

"I had the course on earth. Before we got here."

"I know that, Gilbert." Gnoza drawled out his name in an exaggerated familiarity that made Gilbert want to hit him. "I know all about you."

"Who the hell are you?"

"I'm your guardian angel. I'm going to give you a job. Don't insult me—you're not bright enough."

Gilbert stood up, furious.

"Now, now, Gilbert." Gnoza shook his head at him and his eyes seemed suddenly cold, dark, and strange. "Temper, temper. You need a job like you need to breathe. Remember, Roni's got a job. You don't."

The words pinned him back into the chair as if he were a prized butterfly. They echoed inside him. It was true. Every word was loaded with truth. He felt as if he floated over an abyss inside himself.

Gnoza leaned forward, a strange alien creature looking up at him. "That's better. A pointed truth is an honest knife. That's a proverb of my people. I know you better than you know yourself. You love working. You live for it. You go crazy without it. It's how you keep yourself alive."

"You—" croaked Gilbert. "You're hypnotizing me. Drugging me."

Gnoza smiled, and he was just a misshapen dwarf. He shook his head. "Don't be stupid. I

141

don't need to. These are just words, but the right words.''

Gilbert felt as if his life were turning on the edge of a knife. It was like a vision: every moment of his life, centered around what he did.

"It will be good, working for me. I'll work you hard. And I promise you: the task will be worth it. You will have something to leave Ira." Gnoza's smile disappeared. ''Another proverb: the actions of a man's life are like slow lightning; the longer before it strikes, the greater the burn.''

"What does that mean?''

"Does it matter? Do you want the job?''

He felt glad tears run down his face. He had felt worthless for so long. "I hate you,'' he said softly.

Gnoza looked at him a long time.

Gilbert dried his eyes. Calm descended on him. ''You son of a bitch.''

"You will work for me?'' Gnoza's eyes glowed.

"I'll work for you. How did you do this to me?''

Gnoza didn't speak for a long time. ''I believe in fairies.'' He clapped his hands suddenly and laughed, startling Gilbert. ''Don't you?''

You had to work. You had to build something. That's what Gilbert always says.

"Hold still, please,'' said the technician near her. The nametag read ''BROWN''. Technician Brown was frowning, watching a display. Roni made herself relax.

"That's right. Calm down," said Technician Brown, smiling ingenuously and vacuously. "Okay. Let's disconnect her."

This was real. She was here.

"Calm down, please, Mrs. Bloom."

Roni looked up into Physician White's face. His face was too close. Too close. She pushed him away and stood up unsteadily. "What happened?"

"Your shift is over. It's been eight hours. Are you feeling all right?"

"I feel pretty weak. I had a funny dream."

Physician White helped her to a big stuffed chair and sat on a stool next to her. "Feeling weak is common after a shift. It takes a few minutes for the brain to become fully reconnected. It's nothing to worry about. You just *think* you had a dream, Mrs. Bloom."

Nothing to worry about—she tried to read something in his face but could find nothing but professional concern.

"What are you talking about?"

White leaned back and smiled again down at her. "We use your body for a control, not your mind. We selectively dampen the activity of the brain with a large magnetic field. It takes a few moments for the brain to reestablish its own rhythm. Nothing to worry about, I assure you. But while you are on shift your brain is not functioning. There couldn't have been a dream."

"What was my brain doing for the last eight hours?"

"Nothing. There was no cortical activity at all."

She shook her head. The fog and the fear were receding now. Maybe it was all right after all. Still, below the surface, she could feel an unreasoning fear pulsing within her.

Physician White must have noticed her trembling. "Would you like to see?"

"See what?"

"The cortical traces." He moved over to one of the consoles and performed some operations hidden from her by his body. Before her, a display appeared. There were lines and shapes inscribed with cryptic signs being written in the air before her. Below them was a cross section of a brain—*her* brain. The lines were flat and the cross section a sullen, constant blue.

"There. You see? No activity at all."

Brain dead. She'd been brain dead for eight hours.

She stood up. "Goddamn it. I quit."

Physician White came over to her. "Ms. Bloom—"

Roni pushed him away and looked at them, the room, the chair. They had no idea. "Goddamn it. I said I quit!" She felt strong again now. Her brain had reestablished something, anyway. Her fear dulled into a sullen anger.

She slapped the door and it sprang open away from her. "Goddamn it to hell. Find some other zombie."

Back up Main Street. They'd changed the graphics. Now, instead of various pictures of

Workers Across the World, it seemed to be Great Moments in History. The signing of the Declaration of Independence, the Magna Carta, the Constitution, dozens of people putting pen to paper, signing paper into law.

"Isn't there anybody real here?" she screamed at the Signing of the IPOB Charter. "Isn't there one goddamned human being on this entire fucking ship?" She kicked at the wall. "Talk to me! Answer me!" The Boston signers ignored her, speaking silently to one another in the middle of a vast ballroom.

Work, Gilbert always said. You got to work.

"I hate this place! Do you hear me? I want my son back. I want to go home." She stumbled past the Signing of the Loophole Treaty with Bishop 24 and Bishop 24 presiding over the creation of Venture Capital into the lift.

You got to build something.

"What the hell are we doing here?" she said wearily to the rain forest through which the lift slowly rose.

Gilbert stepped out of the other lift as she entered their home corridor.

"Hey, Roni," he said cheerfully. "Wait till you hear what happened."

Inside the home corridor the blizzard was still silently howling.

"What?" She watched the wolves. They watched her back, red eyes against a white, white snow.

"I got a job."

Everything has to work for a living, Gilbert said. Even wolves. We're no exception.

"Roni?"

"Is it a good job?"

The wolf paced them as they walked towards the apartment. It howled its silent cry. Its tongue was red and its teeth blended into the blizzard and the white of its fur so that it was a blizzard with teeth and tongue.

"What demented bastard is running this place?" She turned on Gilbert. "Will you tell me that?"

"Christ, Roni!" He looked around them. "This *is* a little strange."

"Strange! It's hell on ice."

"So what!" flared Gilbert. "I got a job. You got a job. We're going to survive this and get down onto the Station and make a fortune. That's what we're here for. That's what this is all about. Then, we'll have something."

"Money. We'll have money."

"More than money! We'll have built something."

She laughed. "Something like this graphic? Great. Just great."

"Roni! You don't understand. I got a *job*! A real job. This isn't kitchen work or growing grubs down in food preparation. This is a real job. Hunting something in the ring."

She stopped outside their door. The wolf sat on the snow and wagged its tail, scratched its ear. She remembered the dream. "Hunting for what?"

Gilbert looked uncomfortable. "I don't know."

"Who hired you?"

"This little dwarf named Gnoza."

"A dwarf? You mean an alien, right?" She shook her head. *Aliens.* What the hell did an alien want with Maxwell Station? "They want you to work for them?"

"Right. Gnoza—"

"That doesn't make sense! Why do they want to hire *you*?"

"Damn it!" he shouted. "Because I'll give them a damned good job."

She looked at him, thin, gaunt almost. His glasses were chipped on one lens and their frames were bent. "Why didn't they hire their own team before they left earth?"

"They probably knew people were out here. What difference does it make?"

Roni shook her head. "They could have brought anybody they wanted to. It doesn't take any time to get here in the Loophole. They could bring their own alien team. A team that could do anything they wanted."

"But we're here—"

The ship that came in, the ship in the dream, was the alien ship. She *knew* that. "So what? They sent a whole ship here. They're outfitting a ship in the ring."

"How do you know that?"

"Never mind how I know it. The cost of a team is minimal." She shook her head again. "They need to keep quiet for some reason. And they need people—right. Humans have the rights here. You'd need humans to do it nice and legal and quiet. And dangerous—but they know we're up against the wall." It rang true. "Don't do it, Gil. God knows what they want out there. Stay here. We'll work something out . . ."

Her voice died as she saw Gilbert's face. It was tired, a pale, desperate weariness.

"No. I'm taking the job."

"But, Gil, you don't even know what it is you're looking for."

Gilbert shrugged. "I don't care. I've got to work or I'm going to go nuts. I *want* to work. I *need* to work. The last year has been a screaming hell." He shuddered. "I didn't know how bad it was until Gnoza offered me the job. Hell, you've got a job. Why shouldn't I?"

A job. I've got a job all right. I go brain dead and float over my frozen son for eight hours. I listen to his thoughts, electricity sparking through the ice. *But he's real,* she cried out to herself, *it wasn't a dream. I can talk to my son.*

"It can't be worth it," she said dully.

"Yes it can." He grinned without humor. "I have it on the highest authority."

Silence fell between them. "I have to ship out with Gnoza in a couple of hours. I should be back in a couple of weeks—I'll make enough on this we can wait out the bureaucrats. We can take it easy until the Station opens."

She stared at him. "But we won't." The wolf watched them both.

He looked back at her steadily. "No. We won't. We're not that kind."

"Come on." She opened the door of their apartment and led him in. She didn't turn on the light. She just changed the couch into bed mode.

Sometime later, she let him hold her, then let him get dressed. When he was packed she grabbed him.

"Gil," she said in a taut voice. "You be careful. I have a bad feeling—you come back. You hear? Don't take any chances or I'll—" She buried her face in his hand, then pulled back. "You just come back."

He grinned at her. "Right. A few weeks. Piece of cake."

"Right."

He was gone for several minutes before she made the call.

"Yes? Physician White, please. This is Roni Bloom. I'd like to see if I can get my job back. I was very upset when I left—Yes, I am sorry about that. I can? Good. I'll see you tomorrow."

You had to work. You had to build something.

The first thing Gilbert noticed about Gnoza's ring shuttle was the absence of wall graphics. Nowhere were active murals depicting the joy of work, the love of duty. Nowhere were the logos of Venture Capital and Exterior Developments. There was no blizzard, no white wolves.

The second thing he noticed was just how ludicrous the little alien looked in his suit, a set of five bulging pink balloons, a single transparent balloon over Gnoza's head. He tumbled out of the airlock, seemingly lost forever, then came to a dead stop twenty or thirty meters outside, upright and facing them. "Okay. Send out the broomstick kit first."

"Jesus, he's good," whispered Joe Skald.

"Yeah." Gilbert was grinning.

"Come on, punks. I ain't getting any younger," yelled Gnoza.

"Reminds me of Toby Fitzpatrick. That same clever wit. You ever work for him?"

The broomstick came disassembled in a large bundle. They untied it. Gilbert grunted as he gave it a push towards the airlock. "Can't say I've had the pleasure."

"They have similar charming personalities. I think Toby is a little sweeter. Mind the snug lines—I'm attached to my arms and legs and aim to stay that way."

The tool bundle floated through the airlock. As it moved slowly away from the ship, Gilbert and Joe checked its movement with the snug lines until it floated next to Gnoza. Gnoza started assembling equipment. "Are you going to admire the scenery or come work, eh?"

"Yeah," said Joe reflectively. "I never knew just what to do with Toby when I worked for him. But now, I have the benefit of years of experience."

"Okay," said Gilbert. "What should we do?"

"Drown him. Drown him *now*."

Gilbert laughed. It was good, so good, to be working again.

They pulled themselves along the snug lines until they reached Gnoza. Without comment, Gnoza handed them each snap fittings. "Goes to the main shaft. It should be obvious."

It was, and in a couple of hours, the broomstick was assembled: a long rocket core with four wire seats for each suit.

"Who else is coming?" asked Gilbert pointing at the empty seat.

"No one," said Gnoza. "We'll use that for equipment.

The plan was to find certain large asteroids in the ring with the shuttle and use the broomstick to search each one. Joe and Gilbert were Gnoza's hands. The alien would monitor them through instruments on their suits. This particular asteroid was the first.

"How are we going to know what it is if we find it?" complained Joe. "You don't tell us shit."

"Gentlemen, I wouldn't want to prejudice your fine judgment." Gnoza laughed. "You'll know."

"This guy gives me the creeps sometimes," muttered Joe.

"A frightened human is an observant human," said Gnoza cheerily. "Let's get to work."

They triggered the broomstick and began to search the nearer asteroids. A sense of relaxed alertness pervaded Gilbert. Maybe Gnoza was right. Maybe he *would* know what it was they were looking for when he found it. He felt good. Remember this feeling, he thought. Remember this for Ira. This is a story to tell your son, riding a broomstick through the ring, working like a bastard, searching for something hidden.

It was the only place in the entire *Proud Mary* that Roni knew there would be no graphics. Its inhabitants were a cold, distant people.

They should be. They were frozen.

It was cold down here. Damned cold. Her breath made frost around the rim of her hood. Roni followed the wall: plate after plate, bearing name and medical history. *Berkowitz, Kimberly; Bertini, Rostal; Bloom, Ira.* After that, another set of names.

Gilbert had been gone three weeks. For three weeks, she had wandered the corridors half a ghost when she was off shift, a complete ghost when she was on shift. They had spoken to each other every couple of days but they had not really talked. The ring shuttle was too small for privacy and Gilbert had always been awkward when talking on the job. She had to *talk* to somebody.

But if Ira could hear her, here, now, what would he say to her? A three-year-old child?

I'm here, Mama.

Roni started. "What?"

There was only a frozen silence.

What did she expect?

She felt foolish and embarrassed. "Well, then." Roni sat down on the floor in front of Ira's chamber. "Let's see. What can I tell you?"

Roni suddenly remembered accompanying her mother, Bethel, to the family grave in Quincy, to where Roni's grandmother was buried. Her mother, a stout woman, had sat down cheerfully next to Roni and the tombstone and pulled out a picnic lunch. After lunch was over, she had thought for a long time and began conversing with Roni's grandmother. "Let's see," she had begun. "What can I tell you?"

Maybe he was dead. Maybe the visions she was seeing on shift were dreams, the ship a coincidence. Frozen down to almost nothing, if the spark died in Ira would she feel it? She tried to look in Ira's ice-rimed window but saw nothing. The window was frosted on the inside.

"No," she said softly. "You're not dead." She would know. It would be terrible for him to die, to have been dead all this time, and not to know.

"I got a letter from your Aunt Sara today. Let me read it to you." She opened the printout and began to read, gaining strength from hearing her sister's words, sentences so short and real they brought earth home to her:

" 'Dear Roni, whatever possesses you to stay out there anyway is beyond me. But that's none of my business, I guess. If you need some money, holler. I'll do what I can. Nothing much is happening here. I started working the Skyline job for Toby Fitzpatrick. What a slavedriver he is . . .' "

The letter went quickly. No news from IPOB at her end. She promised to go downtown and ask. The Skyline project would last until spring, she thought. Mike had quit sending child support and she hadn't been able to contact him.

Roni put the letter down and began to cry. Things were so strange and lonely. Gilbert was away on some alien fool's errand. She was marking time on a job that scared her. Her only companion was the memory of her child. Coming here had been a mistake. Ira was frozen, a block of child ice inside a steel tomb. This wasn't the sleeping chambers. The deck was mislabled. This was the catacombs.

Hush, Mama. Hush.

A child's voice. Was she crazy? She didn't care.

"Yes, honey," she whispered.

Her son was alive. He had to be. She would not let it be otherwise.

Roni touched the steel on the outside of Ira's tomb. It was so cold, it tore the skin from the tips of her fingers. The blood froze as it touched the wall but Roni didn't notice.

The three of them ate in a small kitchen near the stern of the ship. Only the hold lay between them and the engines.

Joe frowned at his lasagna. "Why the hell can't they have better food on the Mary?"

Gilbert shrugged. "Maybe when there are more people awake."

Joe grunted. "It'll be a cold day in hell before that happens."

They had been searching asteroids for a month. First, the long search by radio and probe to see if any asteroid met with Gnoza's approval. Then, because it seemed every asteroid *did* meet

with his approval, they jumped on the broomstick and went out to take a look for themselves.
They would orbit the asteroid several times and
Gnoza would call it whether to continue to the
next or stop here for a while. They had actually
landed on a surface—any surface—three times.

Gnoza smacked his lips over the fruit he ha-
bitually ate. The fruit had a sweet, faintly rotting
smell to it. At first, neither Joe nor Gilbert had
been able to stomach it but over the last couple
of weeks they had gotten used to the smell.

Gilbert poked one green and yellow
globe. "What's that taste like?"

"Try it," said Gnoza, grinning. "You might
like it."

"It won't poison me, will it?"

"It might make you puke." Gnoza shrugged
speculatively. "Try it. I'd like to see if it would."

"Thanks, no." Gilbert felt edgy. "Are we getting any closer to whatever the hell it is we're
looking for?"

"Can't say," said Gnoza absently, carefully
shredding something that looked like a melon
and eating the rind.

"How far are we from the Mary?" Gilbert
leaned back and looked at the ceiling.

Joe watched him closely. "Maybe a week
away."

"I don't think I can do my job without knowing a little more."

"Me, neither," said Joe promptly.

Gnoza sputtered. It was one of the sweetest
sounds Gilbert had ever heard.

"I have a contract. If you don't—I'll—"

Joe began humming "Joe Hill" and it was all Gilbert could do to keep from busting right out laughing.

I'll be damned, thought Gilbert. The bugger's turning blue.

Gnoza's face had become a bright, apoplectic blue. Just as suddenly as it came, the color faded except for his eyes. All expression faded with it until Gnoza's eyes were shiny, as if they were painted on his face. Gilbert felt chilled. Gnoza's eyes burned, but they were as cold as the slotted eyes of goats, the flat eyes of fish. It came to him how little he knew here, how little it had taken to bring him here.

"I'll sue you for breach of contract," Gnoza said calmly, coldly.

"Go ahead." Gilbert nodded. "You have to go back to the *Proud Mary* for another crew. That's a week lost. Then a week back here. Two weeks wasted just for not telling me what it is we're looking for. Plus any time it takes to find some warm bodies to replace us."

Gnoza began methodically to break the tough ceramic plates with his fingers. Gilbert was queasy at how much strength lay in those long-fingered hands. What had he started? Gilbert looked over him at Joe. Joe shrugged. It was Gilbert's show. Joe was just following Gilbert's lead.

"God*damn* it!" roared Gnoza suddenly and threw his broken plate against the wall. He stared after it, suddenly silent and still.

"Look, Gnoza." Gilbert leaned forward across the table. "What's so bad about telling us about it? Is it treasonous? Is it dangerous?"

Gnoza looked at him. "Asshole. It's illegal. Maybe. Dangerous? I don't know. It all depends. *Chamcha* and *Rhamcha*."

"What's that?"

"That's what this is all about." Gnoza slammed his fist down on the table. "*Chamcha*: to choose the moral sacrifice. *Rhamcha*: to choose the Holy Sacrifice."

"What the hell are you talking about?"

Gnoza gave Gilbert a long baleful stare. "We are acting out a mitzvah. A penance. A religious obligation. You should be grateful to be given the chance to do God's holy work."

Gilbert shook his head. "I'm lost."

"You don't even know what these things are? I piss on your foul language. It doesn't fit at all. They are *your* words, human. And you, uneducated lout of a man, don't even know what they mean?" Gnoza stood up from the table and suddenly the dwarf looked large to them, a towering personality of rage. "I am under a holy obligation—to find a thing for my master," he said softly. "I don't know what it is either."

He looked at them both, one after another, and he seemed inconsolably sad. "But you do. So I was told."

"This is crazy!" exploded Joe.

"Yes," said Gnoza sternly. "That's what *I* said."

"Who told you?"

Gnoza turned slowly to Gilbert. "I am under no obligation to answer you. My master said to guide you to a section of the ring. After that, he said you would find it for me."

Joe slammed his fist on the table. "This is crazy. Let's take what we've earned and head on back. This is a waste of time."

Gilbert waved him quiet. "Gnoza. How were we supposed to find it?"

"A miracle, of course. Don't be stupid." Gnoza reached over and grabbed Gilbert by the front of his coveralls. "But why you and not me? I believe. I've been faithful all my life. I've done holy work before this. It is I who should have been so chosen. You misbegotten son of a whore worm, why couldn't it have been me?"

She dances along the skin of the Proud Mary, *her arms held above her. She tries to leap into the sky among the stars, but her feet are held fast to the deck. She cannot leave.*

She can feel Gilbert out there. She calls out to him, but he cannot hear her. Only her son can hear her and answer her.

As she walks towards the engines (hazy glow spitting sparks) she can feel someone watching her. Someone that isn't, as a darkness is not merely the absence of light. It frightens her. The presence does not move or make itself known to her. It only watches.

The waiting becomes too much to bear. "Show yourself," she cries. "If you're going to come, come on!"

She crams her fist in her mouth, the stars wheeling above her. The presence has heard her. She knows it. Don't, she says silently. I didn't mean it. I didn't mean it—

The room washed into existence around her in muddy grays and blues. Roni was nauseated. Technician Brown efficiently uncoupled her various connections to the machines. Physician White was watching her warily. There was an old bruise on the side of his face. Roni didn't remember doing it, but she did remember coming to herself standing, with him lying on the floor.

She had felt good. She remembered that, too.

But since then, the straps had stayed on a full five minutes after they disconnected her.

"I'm okay," she said. "I feel fine."

Physician White nodded briefly and technician Brown unbuckled the straps. Roni stood and rubbed her wrists. She took a step toward Physician White and said "Boo!" suddenly.

The man flinched.

Roni laughed and left through the big double doors.

Back in their apartment, her good mood left her and she fidgeted, waiting for Gilbert to call. He was due this afternoon.

Right on time, the display unit chimed.

"Go ahead," she said.

Gilbert's face filled the air before her. "Hi, Ron."

She smiled at him. "Hi, Gil. What's happening?"

"Nothing much. Status quo. Copacetic."

Roni sat up. That didn't sound like Gilbert. "What's going on?"

"Well, we found out Gnoza doesn't know what we're looking for either. It'll take a miracle for us to find it." He laughed. "Literally."

"What do you mean?"

"Exactly—*exactly*—what I said. That's what Gnoza expects to happen to us."

Roni held herself. "So you're coming back, right? It's a wild-goose chase, right?"

"It's easy money. Why should we come back right away?" Gilbert looked off screen for a moment. "Gnoza wants me to get back to work."

"Tell him to go screw. Gil, I don't like you going off and doing something dangerous."

Gilbert looked at her and she couldn't read him at all.

"Gnoza is on a religious quest, he says. He calls what we're doing holy work. If we do this in good faith, a miracle is bound to occur." Gilbert laughed. "He has me half convinced. Anyway, I'm going to stay out here a while longer. The more I make, the better chance we'll have when the Station is finally open." He looked off screen again.

"Gilbert!"

"Maybe a miracle will happen. You wouldn't want me to miss that, would you?"

"Come home, honey," she pleaded. "Come home now."

"Can't quite yet," he said. "But I miss you. I have to go. I'll call again tomorrow."

His face disappeared in fading color.

"Goddammit!" shouted Roni.

She paced around the room. Religion! Men! They were all idiots.

Aliens!

Maybe Gnoza had drugged him. Or hypnotized him. Or something. Who the hell was Gnoza, anyway?

She queried the display unit for a list of different kinds of aliens and got nowhere. In the thirteen years since the landing, hundreds of kinds of aliens had come to Boston. Who they were and what they were was usually known to IPOB, but not always. Even if they were, she had no special access to IPOB files.

The aliens had come with vastly superior technology and an ignorance, intentional or not, of the concept of customs and immigration. Like the Sh'k, who brought a huge ark filled with the otterlike Phneri and blew it up over Boston. The air had been filled with millions of Phneri, falling endlessly, screaming, most dying, some living. Giant rats falling from the sky.

Roni shuddered. Sara had never understood why Roni had first gone into the merchant marine, then leaped at this chance.

Sara had been seventeen when they'd bombed Hull. For years after, a day did not pass without her remarking on it, on the stupidity of their parents for not running.

Roni felt differently. She'd been fifteen and the horror of the bombing was tempered with remembering her father push her out the door, her mother helping her down the street, and then leaving Roni to Sara so that Bethel could return to her husband. Roni had not been surprised. Bethel coming with them would have meant leaving their father. Roni had never been able to imagine them apart. She had said goodbye to them at that moment.

But the fall of the Phneri: falling, body after body, twenty- and thirty-pound rat missiles striking all around the boat. Crashing into the metal deck with a sickening crunch, shattering the mast and rigging, impaled on the antennas and screaming, lashing at her as she tried to push it off, *push it off!*

She was never able to feel safe under an open sky again.

Aliens. She hated them. And now her husband was working for one.

But which one? More and more, it seemed to her that Gnoza had to be a front for someone else. Who?

She tapped into the library of the *Proud Mary* and came up with nothing. There were no aliens referenced that resembled Gnoza. But one thing did appear. All of the articles she queried showed that the aliens were not an amorphous mass of nonhumans, but power blocs. Some of the blocs were entirely earthbound—like the Phneris. Earth was the only planet the Phneris had; the Sh'k had evicted them from their own. Most of the important ones were local examples of blocs that existed across all the Loopholes. The Targives, for instance, had bought up the condemned land in Southie and built their warrens and factories there. No one had ever seen them. They had begun selling ingenious bioengineered animals and plants on the open market.

The life-support system in the *Proud Mary* was Targive-built. She shuddered. She'd never made the connection before now.

The Sh'k were another winner. Unlike the Targive who seemed to prefer mystery, the Sh'k would not inconvenience themselves unless necessary. It was they who dropped the Phneri on Boston. Boston was landfill as far as they were concerned. Their companies were based on beautiful mechanisms, waldoes and robots.

For a moment, she could see these trading empires, buying and selling, making and breaking whole planets and peoples, iceberg-sized, a small piece threading down from the dark, through Boston and back into space.

Roni rubbed her face with her hands. Humans were so small. How did we ever think we'd be able to cope with this?

They were in charge now: Joe and Gilbert. Gnoza showed them how his instruments worked. They were essentially monitors tuned to the brains of Joe and Gilbert. Gnoza was looking for some special excitement or activity. He'd seen nothing.

"Okay," Gilbert had said. "Here's how we do it. To hell with this checking out each and every asteroid. We plot a search pattern to do a long search on every likely asteroid in the area

Gnoza gave us. Then, if we find anything weird, we take the shuttle near it for a closer look. If *that* looks good, we use the broomstick. I'm tired of all this suit work.''

"Me, too," rumbled Joe.

"You could say that again. I hate that god-damn suit," said Gnoza forcefully.

"How come?" asked Gilbert.

"It looks ridiculous. Pink balloons. Feh! I wouldn't wear the damned thing but it was the best the Sh'k could do this far from home. They know *nothing* of esthetics.''

Joe chuckled and Gnoza glared at him.

"How will we tell what's weird?" Joe looked at Gnoza. Gilbert followed suit.

"Don't look at me, gentlemen," said Gnoza dryly. "It's your show. How are *you* going to tell an anomaly?''

Gilbert and Joe turned to each other.

"If it looks like a duck, talks like a duck, and walks like a duck," said Gilbert, "what is it?''

"Ordinary," said Joe promptly. "And we skip it.''

"Right," agreed Gilbert. "Life's too short."

"Huh?" grunted Gnoza. "What the hell are you talking about?''

"Duck hunting," said Joe seriously. "It's a human thing. You wouldn't understand.''

"Assholes," muttered Gnoza.

A week later they had covered fifty great hunks of nickel-iron.

"At this rate, we'll be done next month," said Joe one morning.

"Yeah." Gilbert stared at the various monitors.

"You don't sound real happy."

"It's just . . ." He shrugged. "I think I half believed the little twerp. Wouldn't it be great to be right there at a miracle?"

Joe laughed. "A romantic. I would never have believed it. Not for me, buddy. I read my Bible a long time ago and as far as I can tell, the best place to be when a miracle occurs is somewhere else."

One of the monitor units tolled a bell.

"What is it?" Joe watched the visual above their head.

Gilbert checked the displays. "Anomaly on one of the birdies. Some odd discoloration."

"It's natural, right?"

"I once knew a guy who liked food additives, the way they spiced things up, the funny colors. He convinced himself that everything was natural." Gilbert brought up the image and enhanced it.

"That's a no, isn't it?"

"How would I know? I don't like food additives." Gilbert phased two other displays into the first one. The resulting image showed bars and checks on the surface of the asteroid. "But I think we have to go look at this one. Go get Gnoza."

"Damn." As Joe left the room he stopped. "Is this a miracle? I mean, this is awfully easy."

Gilbert laughed. "Somebody—Gnoza's 'master'—knew there was something here. He knew about where it was and he knew we could find it. With all that, there's no miracle in finding it.''

''That's what I was afraid of. It makes me wonder what he thought the miracle would be.''

The rotation of the asteroid took the anomaly away from them as they approached. As they came close to it, the checks and bars turned towards them.

Gilbert whistled.

''You ain't kidding,'' said Joe.

Gnoza was silent.

The checks and bars were the remains of buildings and other structures, clearly artificial. Both Joe and Gilbert turned on Gnoza.

''What *is* this?'' cried Gilbert.

''I don't like it. I don't like it one little bit.'' Joe chewed on his lower lip.

Gnoza didn't answer them immediately. ''I'm not sure. It might be—''

''What's it doing now?'' yelled Joe.

Part of the structure facing them shimmered and seemed to change shape. Geometric patterns raced across its surface, became three-dimensional structures.

''—the relic of a war,'' said Gnoza softly.

''*A war!* For chrissakes!'' Gilbert pushed himself out of the monitor console over to the pilot instruments. He slapped the Attention button and started keying in commands.

''A *big* war,'' muttered Gnoza, staring at the movement on the surface of the asteroid. There was a dark pyramid pulsing on the surface now.

"Some miracle, Bloom!" Joe looked at Gilbert, then back at the screens. There was a faint flash on the pyramid and a sense of darkness, beating like a great heart, rushing at them. "Some fucking—"

Gilbert felt rather than saw a flash—for a moment he could see the bones deep in his hands as he tried to type in commands.

Then, nothing.

She was half drunk. Tonight, she would go the rest of the way.

A large vodka and orange juice was on the table before her. Around her, she tried to read the various notices pinned to the walls of the bar. They were graphics. They had to be. Who the hell would pin paper to the wall?

It was for atmosphere.

Christ.

"I've had it," she said to the drink, then drained it. "I don't care anymore. What the hell's the point? Are we going to make a *home* down there? This was a crazy idea."

It was Gilbert's fault. Asshole. Out there looking for something crazy. "Asshole," she muttered. She lay her head on the table and sobbed. She missed her son. She missed Gilbert. She missed trees and lakes and birds. God, she was tired of this place.

For a moment, she thought she heard a distant, faraway cry, but then it was gone.

"Nope. I'm going to live in the real world, now. No more dreams." She ordered another drink and the service unit brought it to her table. She drank part of it.

She remembered the darkness in the last dream. Waiting for her. Looking for her.

The whole fucking world was out to get her, from the falling Phneri to the cops that bombed her parents. No more. She wasn't going to run any more.

"I know where you are," she yelled and stood up. The table turned over with a crash, and she swayed as she stood. There was no one else in the bar.

"There's never anybody else around. Never anybody else but you. I know you're watching me. Come out and face me. Come out, come out, wherever you are."

The door to the bar opened suddenly. The lights streamed in behind the figure who came into the bar. She couldn't see who it was. The figure walked jerkily towards her. The room swam around her. She closed her eyes and opened them. The room was no steadier.

"Give me a deboozer!" she whispered to the servant. "A fast one."

The service unit gave her a fizzing drink and she drained it.

There was a soundless explosion between her ears and a roaring through her mind. The world split apart and fused back together in focus, steady, glittering. Everything had a hard edge to it.

The figure stopped before her.

"Bishop 24," it said in a faint, dry voice. "At your service."

It was a dream. He knew it was a dream.

He was sitting in one of those old Victorian loveseats, where only two people can sit and the seats face opposite ways. He was facing one way. The person in the other seat was facing another.

He looked to the other person, expecting it to be Roni but it was Toby Fitzpatrick. He knew it was Toby, even though Toby had Joe's face.

"Better drown me now," he said seriously.

Gilbert looked around. He was in a crystal room. Roni was standing a few feet away.

"Get out of the seat, Toby," he yelled. "It's not for you. Get out of it."

"Better drown me. It's the only way."

Gilbert stood and grabbed Toby, tried to pull him out of the chair. Toby was stuck fast.

"Drown me, *now*."

"You son of a bitch! You don't belong here. This place is special. This place is never, ever for you!" And he pulled with all his strength. Roni was suddenly there and laid a hand across both of his.

Slowly, slowly, Toby came out of the chair, looking mournful and resigned all at once.

"Okay," Toby said. "If you want it that bad."

And he was gone.

Roni was standing so close to him he could smell her, as if they had just made love. He wanted to cry.

He sat down on his side and looked back at her. He pointed to the other seat.

"That's for you."

She sat down and he was so glad he had to turn away.

He couldn't look away.

He looked at her—

There was a dragon on his shoulders.

Besides that, the Bishop looked like his pictures: great, faceted eyes over a squirming mouth, a body thin enough to support prayer, long wicked arms ending in claws. Under the shallow cylindrical body beneath she could see hundreds of tiny legs. He seemed to be perpetually still. There were only sudden and complete changes. One moment his arm was here, the next there, like an old film. She never saw the movement. *Aliens* . . .

The dragon on his shoulder seemed like a feathered fish, all bright colors and feathers and scales. It seemed asleep. Occasionally, it hissed.

"You're behind this. You sent Gilbert out."

The Bishop nodded. "Yes."

"How much else are you responsible for?"

The Bishop tilted his head to one side and looked at her. "Such a large question."

"The settling of Maxwell Station—"

"—will not go forward until I find what I need to find."

"Why didn't you just find it before?"

The dragon woke and muttered in a high voice. The Bishop reached below the table and pulled out something from a pouch. He held it up by its tail and the dragon seemed to wake up suddenly, and it was gone. The dragon closed its eyes. Roni shuddered.

The Bishop continued: "If I had known then what I now know, it would have happened better. The system was sold through a broker and until the sale was final I did not know what system this was. You see, I thought we still owned it. I thought I had plenty of time."

"*You* owned it?"

"The Centaurs."

"Plenty of time for what?"

"To find what I have lost, of course."

"And what is that?"

The Bishop did not speak for a long time. "I'm here to find a friend, Mrs. Bloom. A friend I betrayed a very long time ago."

"Who?"

"It is a past context, Mrs. Bloom. I don't wish to speak of it."

Roni shook her head. "What the hell is going on? I don't understand any of this. Why all this secrecy?"

"*Chamcha.*"

"What?"

The Bishop didn't speak for a moment. His gaze turned away from her for a moment, though Roni had no idea how she knew that. After a moment, he looked at her and his voice was gentler, as if he were trying to persuade her of something.

"I'm a traitor, Mrs. Bloom. I am selling out my position. I am selling out my people."

"For a friend?"

"Yes."

"I hope this friend is grateful," said Roni caustically. "It's damned near ruined my life and my marriage."

"I betrayed him, Mrs. Bloom." The Bishop shook his head slowly and this time, Roni could see the movement and knew the slowness had to be intentional. "I think he would kill me if he could."

Silence fell between them for a long minute. The dragon yawned and in his mouth were rows of needle-thin teeth quivering of their own accord.

Roni looked at him wearily. "There's more to this, isn't there? Now you want something from me, don't you?"

"Yes. Most assuredly."

"What?"

The Bishop held the dragon tightly and leaned forward to bring his huge faceted eyes down to a level with hers. She could smell him—a spice of saffron and plastic. She saw the quivering movement of his mouthparts and the flickering in each of his thousand tiny eyes.

"I need you," he said at last. "I need you to go to work."

There was a fairy on his helmet.

Gilbert looked at it for a long time, shook his head, and closed his eyes. Looked again.

The fairy was twelve inches tall and had Roni's face. It was looking at him.

He sat up and the fairy tumbled to the floor and was gone. He was in his suit—the last thing he remembered was a tumbling darkness and a flash.

Gnoza sat across from him in a suit, tapping his fingers together rhythmically and crooning.

"Gnoza?" he croaked.

Gnoza looked over to him, slid across the floor to him. "How do you feel?"

"I'm alive. That's more than I expected."

Gnoza nodded. "I put you and Joe in your suits. You were both pretty banged up and the shuttle was leaking air. I hoped you were just unconscious."

"What happened?"

"We were fired upon."

Gilbert stood up. There was a faint gravity. "I know that. Why the hell are we still alive?"

Gnoza didn't answer. He stood up and moved over towards the other suit and looked in the helmet visor. "Joe is still out. Does your suit have medical instruments?"

"Yeah. Let me check them."

"It is a poor design. There should be instructions on the outside. Printed in three or four languages. Maybe the suit should *tell* you what is wrong."

"You can redesign it later if you want to." The instruments said Joe's vital signs were still fine, but he was unconscious. Gilbert shone a light in through the visor. Joe's eyes were closed and his breathing seemed easy.

"Did you move him?"

"I had to put the suit on him, didn't I? Look at your incredibly primitive instruments. We have a vacuum here."

"Great," muttered Gilbert. "Okay. What shot at us?"

"A war relic."

"Come on, Gnoza. Whose war? What war? When was it? What kind of things can we expect here?" Gilbert wanted to shake the dwarf but he didn't know what the suit would take.

Gnoza shook his head miserably. "I don't know. My master—"

"And who is *that*?"

Gnoza looked at him for a long time. "Bishop 24."

"Christ!" Who the fuck knew what the Bishop would do? Eat them, maybe. "It was a Centaur war? With who?"

"I don't know."

"Don't lie to me, Gnoza!"

"I'm not! He only mentioned the Centaurs fought a war here. That's all! I thought we were looking for a lost shrine." Gnoza shook his head. "I didn't expect this any more than you did."

"What kind of a shrine?"

"A religious one—he *is* a bishop." Gnoza beat his hands against the floor. "It is the duty—the *Rhamcha*—of the church to bring the inedible into the world gracefully and safely."

"The 'inedible'?"

174

"Fa'chach'da."

"Fa—what?"

" 'Inedible by reason of insanity.' " Gnoza began tapping his fingers together again.

"Get a grip, Gnoza. What the hell are you talking about?"

Gnoza stopped and looked lost for a moment. "It was the Centaurs, first. They believe everything that isn't sentient is edible. But what are those creatures that are not sentient *yet*? Are they edible? No one knows. Can they compete? Not yet. So they decided to care for such creatures until they become sentient. Humans are not sane, yet." Gnoza looked at him venomously. "I don't think they ever will be."

"I don't like the idea of being food."

"Food never does."

This was getting them nowhere. He looked out one of the ports. They were on the surface of an asteroid, the structures outside told him which one.

"How do you figure we get out of this, Gnoza?"

"You humans are the ones with miracles. You figure it out."

Outside, waving to him, was the fairy again. She kept waving him to come outside.

"You don't have any ideas?"

"None. We can't get off this rock without getting shot down. We couldn't get home if we could, anyway. We have no engines. The relic outside took care of that. How long does your suit last?"

"A day or two."

"Mine will last maybe a week. Want to take a short cut around misery?"

Gilbert turned to the dwarf. "I'll wait a bit, if you don't mind."

Gnoza shrugged. "Just asking. Me, I'll wait a few days to make my peace with God. It takes time for someone like me. I have a lot of praying to do."

The fairy waved to him frantically.

"Throw in one for a miracle," said Gilbert absently.

"I've been doing that for days."

What the hell? "I'm going outside."

"I thought you weren't going to die just yet."

"I've always been an optimist."

Gnoza didn't reply to that.

It took a full minute for the airlock to realize there was no air on either side of it and to open anyway. That minute was the longest Gilbert had ever known.

Do you believe in fairies, Gilbert?

Outside, a twelve-inch Roni was waving to him. He took a deep breath and walked over to her.

"It took you long enough, Gil."

"Roni, what are you doing here? These things ought to be shooting at me, shouldn't they? They shot us down. This is getting too damned—"

"Shut up," she said evenly. "We've got a job to do. Maybe, if we're lucky, we'll even come out of it alive."

He shut up. When you're trusting in a fairy, he thought, that's the sort of thing you do.

She led him over a rill and deep into the shadow of a cliff.

"Up there," she said finally.

He looked up and saw a cave. "What's in it?"

"Let's go." She grunted and started to climb the wall.

Gilbert watched her for a minute and reached down and picked her up. She seemed a little heavy for twelve inches. He put her on his shoulder. "Put on weight since I been gone, sugar?"

"Only you would say that now."

They climbed up to the cave and stood at the lip. Inside was darkness.

"Turn on your light, Gil."

"Oh, yeah." He turned on his headlamp.

The cave looked shallow. It was filled with a cottony substance like cobwebs. He pulled a prybar from his leg pack and touched the cobwebs. They brushed away.

"The real stuff is later, I bet." Roni led the way in.

Gilbert passed through the cobwebs, around a bend in the cave, and into the final chamber. There, tied to the various walls of the chamber by the cobwebs was a large woven object, vaguely egg-shaped, textured like burlap.

"That's it," said Roni sounding satisfied.

"That's *what*?" yelled Gilbert.

"What you've been looking for. What you, Joe, and Gnoza came out here for. I'm just trying to help."

Gilbert wanted to bang his head against the wall. "And what do we do with it *now*?"

"I figure that's up to you."

"You're a big help."

Roni walked over to it, up its front, and looked down on the blank, fuzzy surface. "Wake up!" she cried.

Gilbert could swear he could hear her voice rolling into the distance, rolling to ears that could hear.

"You try," she said.

"Wake up," he said, feeling stupid.

"Try it again. Try it with feeling."

"This is too much," he said. "I banged my head when we were shot at and now I'm crazy. I'm going to unseal right here. It's pointless, right?"

Roni jumped off the lump and ran up the front of his suit, hanging in front of his face by the helmet lights.

"Don't you dare, you miserable bastard! You're my husband and *by God* you'll come back to me if I have to drag you by your thumbs."

They locked eyes. He started to laugh. "What have I got to lose? Look, let's call him together, okay? I mean, I believe in miracles; I believe in fairies." He clumsily tried to clap his hands. "See?"

"You're a dummy," she said softly. "And I love you."

He held her, and together they cried out, and he tried, he really tried, to call out to something sleeping. "Wake up!"

From a great distance, they heard something stir.

Then, he sat down. He was tired. "Roni," he said softly. "I love you and I wish we'd never left earth. I'm sorry to leave you a widow."

He cradled her against his chest and he swore he could feel her tiny head. "Dummy," she said fondly and sadly. "You are such a dummy."

There was a shadow in the light and he looked up. A great thing stood in front of him, all arms and legs and a block and tackle body. Two huge eyes stared down at him. He looked down in his hands and they were empty.

"Okay," he said softly. He looked around the room. Behind them, the egg thing was an empty sack in the darkness. "Right." He looked up into the eyes. "Your move." Skin of a rhino, he thought. Eyes of an elephant.

The alien watched him for a long time, stood straight. He stepped back and gestured to Gilbert to lead.

"Shall we dance?" Gilbert laughed and began to lead him back to the ship.

There was an insistent buzzing in her ears. It made her head ache.

Her head was resting on something hard.

She raised her head and opened her eyes. A service unit was buzzing at her. Where was she?

Roni looked around the room. She was in the bar. Her mind was fuzzy. She looked around again. She came here to get drunk—the way her head hurt, she'd managed that.

"There is a call for you, Mrs. Bloom," said the service unit. "The caller is very insistent."

"I'll take it now." Roni rubbed her face. She didn't remember drinking that much.

Gilbert's face appeared before her.

"Roni," he said and tears were in his eyes. "Oh, Roni."

"What's—" She closed her eyes and opened them again. "How's it going?"

"We're coming home. We found it—him, I guess. Thank you. Thank you for bringing me home."

Roni fuzzily tried to remember what she'd done since the last time they'd talked. "What did I do?" she asked at last.

Gilbert looked at her for a long time. "Everything important," he said at last. "We had an accident, but it's all right now." He stopped and watched her.

It made her nervous. "You know where I am, Gil? I'm in the bar. I got drunk for the first time in years—"

"I miss you, Roni."

She blinked. "I miss you, too, Gil. What kind of an accident? Was it serious?"

"It could have been," he said slowly. "But we found an alien on the asteroid." An excitement filled his voice. "He's big, Roni. And he looks like every animal I've ever seen. It's strange—" He paused.

"Great," she said. *Aliens.*

"You'll like him, I think." Gilbert shrugged.

"He's outside working on the ship. We wouldn't have made it back without him."

They talked a bit more, but Gilbert signed off soon to conserve power. They'd be back in a few days.

Roni returned to their apartment to find a message on their system: Hydroworks would not be needing her services for some time. A new technique was being tried. Enclosed in the message was a funding credit for her shift work.

The credit was far more than she would have made on any given shift, and she wrestled with herself for a few minutes before she decided to take it. She'd hated that job. And she felt deep in her soul she earned that money. Roni decided to think of the extra as a bonus.

The day before Gilbert returned, the word came down from IPOB: Maxwell Station was being opened. The red tape had been cleared away. In hours, the *Proud Mary* went from a ghost ship to being filled with activity. They'd be starting to land on the planet in just a few weeks. Ira would be thawed by the time Gilbert came home.

And Gilbert and Roni were first in line.

Ira had been cranky and Roni prayed he wouldn't start crying. Still, Roni felt good. An alien was bringing Gilbert home, and she was prepared to like any creature that would do that. As she waited, she thought over how much she had to tell Gilbert when he stepped through the public airlock. The words were crowding through her. They came together and then they were gone. There was nothing there but Gilbert. Nothing was more important than that. She grabbed him and kissed him and held him and Ira together for a long minute. They released one another slowly.

She looked at Ira and Ira wasn't looking at Gilbert or her, but past them both.

There, in the airlock, was a giant: skin like a rhino, eyes like an elephant, the arms of a bear. He was huge and beautiful and to Roni he somehow looked like the breath of home. Ira only had eyes for him.

The creature came over to them.

Gilbert gestured towards him. "Roni, this is Gray."

Gray looked down at her intently, silently, for several seconds. "I know you," he said at last in a deep voice.

Yes. Aliens.

Roni returned his look and smiled. "And I know you."

Hull: 2019

2019 5:34

Peter S. Croix was up with the sun. His home was higher up than the other houses on Hull, but the lot descended in steps to the sea. It was down here, on the south side, near the shade of the sea wall and where the stiff salt smell was close, he tended his garden. It was the only level spot on his property and he worked the soil religiously every morning during the short New England summer. Each spring, he brought in new topsoil to replace the old, salted soil from the winter. And in the gray and blue sunrise, he sprayed the garden with a fine mist—not too much; too much would waterlog the soil—to wash the salt off the leaves.

He planted corn, soybeans, and sometimes a little wheat next to the vegetables: crops grown at home in Saskatchewan. They did poorly but he did not mind.

This morning started hot for New England: in the mid-eighties. The newsnets were already calling this spring the "Hammer of God Heatwave." By noon, the air would be a thick, sweaty, even hundred degrees.

Peter hoed the gray soil. There was already salt rime on the downward side of the wall and he could feel it with his feet: the clinging grittiness of salt in the soil, the tackiness of the handle of the hoe. The sun warmed his bare back, and the ocean seemed to purr faintly against the wall.

Two figures watched him from the shade of the sea wall, both dressed in ancient jackets and leather trousers. They were arguing, but Peter ignored them as he'd been ignoring them for nearly twenty years.

"It's going to happen today. Sometime, today. I cannot tell when," said Louis Riel, fanning himself. "It is too hot here in the south."

"You've been saying that since Batoche," scoffed Gabriel Dumont. "Even before they hung you."

"I had a vision! I saw *God*! He brought us to that place and made us fight for it!"

Gabriel shrugged. "Of course you saw God. In that country, who wouldn't? What else was there to see?"

The sweat ran from Peter's short hair and down

into his eyes. Peter hoed vigorously to drown the two of them out.

"Peter!" cried a new voice, but Peter was trying so hard to ignore Gabriel and Louis he didn't hear it at first. When a man stood in front of him, he was confused and surprised.

It was Frank Cobb with two cups of coffee. "Saw you working out here so early, I thought you might want a cup of something."

Peter nodded gratefully and took one of the cups. "Thought I would get in some work now, then later take the boat out to the Banks for a couple of days. Lat Do told me the other day his men found a run of shad out there. Like to check it out."

Frank didn't answer for a long while. "You don't think anything's going to happen, then?" He gestured towards the sun, still yellow orange. "They've been getting ready for God knows what." Frank moved up the hill out of the garden and turned towards Hog Island to watch it. Peter lay down his hoe and followed him.

In the direction of the sun, Hog Island was backlit, black and factory shaped. The sounds of machinery and activity had been going on since long before sunrise. From here, Peter could hear an occasional shout in Cambodian or Chinese or Polish, and several boats were unloading crates. Hog Island was a smuggling center and as its neighbor he'd heard languages from all over the world.

We're all immigrants here, Peter thought as he sipped the coffee. Salty. Everything here seemed to taste of salt.

"They're up to something, Peter," whispered Louis next to him. "It's going to happen tonight!"

Peter started and stared at him, then turned the stare into a look out to sea. There was nothing but water and a few boats idling in purposefully over the old foundations. These foundations marked the graves of lost houses, washed away by the rising water.

"Yeah, Frank," he said at last. "They're doing something. But the last move isn't up to them; it's up to the Commission. I haven't heard a peep out of them."

"Is that what Lat Do said?"

"I didn't need to ask Lat Do that. It's obvious."

"Did you talk with the Bishop?" asked Frank, looking down as if embarrassed.

"No." Peter walked back down the hill and returned deliberately back to his hoeing.

"You're our chairman in this," said Frank slowly as he followed. He squatted slowly down on his thin thighs to look up in Peter's face. " 'Cause you got connections: both Lat Do and the Bishop listen to you." He took a handful of earth and rubbed it in his hands.

"Don't forget Commissioner James. We're going against the MDC and that's *his* department."

Frank studied the earth in his hands. "Maybe you should ask the Bishop what to do."

"Ask him what, Frank?" Peter hoed furiously. "Ask him if the Metropolitan District

Commissions's going to attack Hog Island? We know the answer: it's yes. IPOB will insist: Lat Do is unregulated competition. I could ask him, when is it going to happen? Then, what's he going to ask *me*? He's going to ask are you staying? Which side are you going to fight on? Boston's? Or Lat Do's? And what am I going to say? Tell me that.''

''Tell him we're trying to keep our homes, Peter.'' Frank stood up and let the earth fall. ''They're poor enough, but they're ours.''

Peter leaned on his hoe. ''Then what do I need to ask him? When? We know when. They're coming today. This afternoon, probably.''

Frank paled. ''You said you were sending out the boat.''

''To the harbor. To moor up—I don't want it getting sunk.''

''You said the shad—''

''That's what I'm telling Lat Do. That's what Bethel and the girls will be doing, if I can get them off this place without you shooting off your mouth.''

''Which side are you on?''

Peter shrugged. ''I don't know.''

Frank shook his head violently. ''It ain't fair. It just ain't fair.''

Peter didn't answer.

Frank sighed. ''I'll get everybody together down at the school. You come on down about noon. We'll figure things out then.''

He turned to go, stopped, and turned back to

Peter. "How do you know? You didn't even ask the Bishop."

Peter saw Louis Riel and Gabriel Dumont stand up and begin walking up towards the house. They'd be looking in on the kids, checking the ammunition and guns.

"I know, Frank," he said as he returned to his hoeing. "I just know. That's all."

1997

It all came down to the river.

The little town of Batoche nestled against the river's banks, along its shores. The river was its food and work, its life and breath. It was timeless, as all rivers are timeless, because they are made of where water is, where land is not, and the pull of gravity. A frozen river is water waiting to be free. This river had flowed down this plain forever, endless water that came from nothing more than rain and became nothing less than the sea. And it came to Peter, sitting on its banks looking down at the water, that there was not enough water in it to wash the blood from his hands.

It was not Doctor Murdock, fresh from the hospital where Marie lay in a coma, sitting next to him. Nor was it Father Pierce, the family priest. Nor some old friend, but Gabriel—who, it must be admitted, was perhaps more and less than a friend.

"No one knows but her," said Peter, watching the slow swells move downstream. A king-fisher shot out of the birches near them and caught a fish, struggled up out of the water to disappear back into the trees.

"About what?" Gabriel picked a grass stem and chewed it.

"You and Louis. Maybe my grandmother, too. She seemed to know something. But she's dead now. My grandmother and my sister. The folks never suspected."

Gabriel laughed softly. "Little Marlena. Her mother died over there, I think." He gestured towards where the bank fell towards the river. "It was late in the afternoon, when we knew the damned British were going to win. Canada. Empire. Company. They were just words for 'British.' We were Metis! Something different. A new nation. Indian, French, Scot, all bred together, all married to one another. We were a light that would change the world." Gabriel shook his head. "Louis wouldn't let me stay. 'God will not let you,' he told me."

Peter did not answer. The pumpkins across the field were brightening in the afternoon light, yellow as brass.

"I could never refuse him," Gabriel murmured. "Not the first time in Fort Garry, when they were going to take the land without ever knowing we were there. 'We shall make a place for ourselves,' Louis said. Or when he had that man executed—what was his name? He had a moustache. A blond man—Irish, I think. Louis tried him and had him killed, and everything fell apart. The amnesty. Everything. I left then—didn't see him again for years. Not until here. I was right there—'' Gabriel pointed down to the docks. ''Right there, when they brought him back up here. We Metis were in trouble again—land claims. As if there were anything else we'd ever had trouble with. Land in Manitoba. Land here. It was always land. And he stepped from that boat onto the docks and looked at me—a chill down to the bone. And he said, 'Gabriel, we are here again. Do you remember?' *Oui, je me souvien.*''

Gabriel laughed dryly. ''And I was ready to lay down my life for him right there. It was my *duty* to give him anything he asked for. Just as it was his duty to send me away and face the English by himself.'' He kicked at the grass furiously and it didn't move. ''Damn them and their red coats, their bright, bright buttons! Damn their arrogance and their gall. To hang him like he was just another criminal. My poor dead friend.''

Peter felt as if he were just underwater, watching the surface recede into the darkness. The light was fading now.

''You know why I looked away?'' he said suddenly to Gabriel.

Gabriel didn't answer.

''I'll tell you.'' Peter leaned back and stared into the darkening sky. ''I was waving to you.''

''Jesus, boy!''

''I wanted you to see us planting the earth *here*. For all those stories you and Louis had ever told me. Louis died in Regina and you were never able to come home, to come here. But we *stayed*. My family had kept our patch. It was like keeping a promise. And right then, Marie and I were planting *our* land. Yours, too. I waved to you and I hit something.'' He shrugged, sat up, turned to Gabriel. ''Maybe a rock. I went back and I hunted all around where it happened. *I didn't find anything*. No rock. No anything. Just me. Just me.'' He stood up. ''I killed her. I killed my sister.''

''Don't. Peter, she's not dead.''

''I saw her in the hospital. One arm gone, the other ruined. Spine broken—not that it matters because her legs are mangled. But the worst''— he rubbed his face—''the worst was when she woke up. She always had this light about her, right? You saw it. It was like sunlight. When she woke up and I saw her, it was gone.''

''She's still recovering. She was probably in a great deal of pain.''

Peter shook his head. ''I know what I know. The light's gone out. I could live with anything but that.''

He stood and dusted himself off, watched the river. It was the river that made the town, coming from darkness and going off into darkness. ''I'm leaving. I can't stay anymore.''

''It was an accident—''

''Not today, but soon. When Marie gets out of the hospital. I'll leave working the farm to Mom and Dad. Then, I'm gone. They can hire help or do it themselves. Mainly, they can look after Marie. I can help with that—send money and all. But I can't stay.''

"Peter!"

"I don't want to talk to you. You don't mean anything to me anymore."

"Peter, for the love of God!"

"This place is just a town by the river," he said slowly, counting the lights coming on one by one. "It doesn't mean anything, anything at all." He turned and walked back towards the house to call the hospital and see how Marie was doing.

Behind him, he heard the sound of an old and lonely man sobbing under the night sky.

2019 7:04

Bethel was waiting for him when he reached the house. He could never leave the bedroom without her waking, though often he didn't know it until later. After he showered, there was coffee waiting for him. He sipped it, wondering if he would start getting calls. The conversation with Frank would spread among the families on the hill quickly.

He looked out the kitchen window. You could see the bones of what Hull had looked like fifty years ago. Two hills connected by a spit of land. A second spit beyond the second hill connecting Hull to mainland Hingham like a man holding a pair of pince-nez with his fingertips.

Boston and the surrounding area had sunk, continued sinking, was sinking *right now*, at this *very minute*. And the two hills were nearly all that was left.

The spit was under six feet of water at high tide and down to two feet when the tide was low. There had been houses there; now only the broken concrete and wood foundations remained. The water was grimy, but at low tide the old roadbed could still be seen and the storms had not yet rusted away the old street signs. This gave it the appearance of a ghost town, whisked away by the sea.

Only Hog Island remained untouched. It had been a small island until World War II, when the army had broadened it and built great concrete reinforcements there and on the hill of East Island and the old watchtower in Peter St. Croix's backyard. After that, Hog Island had gone to town houses, condominiums, and eventually was abandoned as the water continued to rise. It had lain like fallow land until Lat Do had come to claim it.

He shook his head and looked around the room.

Bethel's parents had owned this house and willed it to her. Peter loved the old house in a way Bethel had never understood, loved it as those bereft of land love when land is again theirs.

He'd be damned if he'd let the MDC bomb it to rubble.

"You have any plans today?" he asked casually.

"Not so you'd notice. Figure you might need

me around.'' She leaned back in her chair and stirred her coffee idly. Bethel was a small woman, but built stoutly, with a broad nose, bright blue snapping eyes, and short stubby fingers.

''No. I don't think so. Why don't you take the whaler across over to the mainland and catch the bus into Boston. Take the kids and make a day of it.''

''Things are going to pop today?''

''Am I that transparent?''

''Pretty much.''

''Hm.'' He turned away from the window. ''So much for subtlety. I think I can handle this thing but I want you and the kids out of the way in case something happens.''

Bethel snorted. ''Protect us. Just like you to try to do that.''

''Just for the day.''

''I'll think about it.''

''Damn it, Beth!'' he cried. She looked up at him and pointed a finger at him: *don't start this; I'll finish it*. ''Okay,'' he muttered.

''Did you find this out from the Bishop?''

''No. I haven't talked to the Bishop at all.''

Across the room the phone was attached to the wall, the display unit dark. He knew a call was coming. He hoped he'd be ready for it.

The Bishop's office was in the old parking garage downtown. Eight floors of ramps, block columns, and greasy concrete, sheathed over with plywood; now called Miller's Hall. God knew why the aliens had chosen it—God and maybe Bishop 24.

Peter could not have chosen a more confusing place to house the office of the Most Important Alien on Earth. He capitalized it in his mind and grinned. The grin disappeared. Why did the Bishop agree to see him? *He's not sure yet who's important so he's not taking any chances.* Right. That was probably it.

There was a foyer before the Bishop's office, and at the small desk sat a gnome with a great head and huge blue eyes, busily scanning a display unit. Without looking up, the gnome spoke. "What do you want?"

"I'm Peter St. Croix. I have an appointment with the Bishop."

"Hm," said the gnome noncommittally. "You can call me Gnoza. Did you read the pamphlet IPOB issued?" asked Gnoza suddenly.

"Yeah." Something about Gnoza irritated him but he swallowed it. Peter pulled the pamphlet out of his jacket. " 'So You Want to Meet the Bishop.' Do I really have to worry about him eating me?"

"A lot of people think so. Didn't you see the interview over the net last night?" asked Gnoza, acting surprised. At least, he *might* be surprised. He quit looking in that damned display.

"No. I was out on the Bank, fishing." Peter looked around the room, edgy. "I'm a fisherman."

"I know what you are."

"Yeah. Right." Great. So this was worth the boat ride up from Hull? Maybe he should just go home now. This was a long shot, anyway. "So, is he going to eat me?"

"Probably not." Gnoza turned back to the display. "Don't challenge him. Don't let yourself be tested. And follow his lead. You can go in now. He's ready for you."

"Just like that. Clever guy." There was only one door other than the one he came in, so he opened it and went inside.

"Bishop?" Peter didn't see him immediately. The dust of cheap paint on plywood seemed to be everywhere, and underneath it the thick smell of cars and a faint spice.

"Sit down, Mister St. Croix." The Bishop's voice was dry sticks and rattled as he talked. The voice came from the other side of the wall.

Peter sat in a soft chair. He could hear a rustle from around the partition and he tried to look. A blur and the Bishop stood behind his desk.

For a moment, Peter just looked, then he looked away. After a moment, he forced himself to look back. This is the guy you came to see, he told himself.

The Bishop was all claws and insect eyes, and he had a small—young, maybe?—dragon perched on his shoulder. But somehow—this was the crazy part—he *looked* like a bishop. He had that same sort of kingly grace and authority Peter was used to seeing in a bishop. It was the way he stood, firm and high, and the way he seemed to be looking at you: it wasn't just him; it was the entire church watching. Peter suddenly felt embarrassed that this was his office; embarrassed for humanity that it should show such small courtesy to him. *He must have chosen this place—we would have had him staying in one of the hotels.*

Bishop 24 cocked his head, gestured gently towards him. "Many humans would rather talk to me in the dark. We can turn the light off if you want."

Peter sat up straight. By God, he wouldn't *look* afraid, anyway. At least he could keep up appearances.

"No, thank you, sir. I'll talk to you like this, if you don't mind."

The Bishop just looked at him for a long time. "You want me to help refinance the Hingham Reclamation Project."

Peter nodded. "The old project died in the depression. That was in 2008."

Bishop 24 nodded. "I'm familiar with it."

Right. Of course right. "Yeah. We've been trying to get funding ever since. Y'see, when Boston sank, a lot of little projects got started to help the sea level communities from getting drowned out. We live in Hull—we bought there because the HRP financed our mortgage. That came to a stop seven years ago. That'd be okay, usually, because by then we had a good part of the mortgage budgeted, y'see. Most of us did, anyway." He had to make the Bishop see. His kids had grown up on dry land instead of on a fishing boat because of the HRP. It was important—more than some damned alien—

For a brief moment, he remembered hearing about the aliens landing, fishing out on the Bank. He couldn't see Boston, but he'd been watching those strange cloud formations for hours, boiling up, settling down, like gray fog fountains. He'd called Bethel to see if she and the kids were all right. She'd barely been able to talk from excitement.

—more than *any* alien business. Peter cleared his throat. "But the water keeps rising. It's risen nine feet since then. The lower houses are washed out. And the higher ones, like mine, need the walls raised. We can take care of ourselves, but we need help holding back the sea."

His voice trailed off. The Bishop had begun pacing back and forth. He held his claws together and seemed to be fiddling his—fingers? could they be called fingers?—together rhythmically. It was like watching an abbot pace with a rosary.

The Bishop stopped abruptly and turned in a blur and leaned over the desk. Peter shrank away.

"How did you come here?"

"I took a boat from Hull—"

"No. That's not what I meant." The Bishop was absolutely still for a moment. "I've been adult for nearly four of your centuries and every day here I feel as if I had just been hatched. I feel blind, deaf, among you.''

"Sir—"

"I speak forty-two earth languages fluently. There are an additional twenty I can read. I have constructed a corporate directorship that must stand against any legality any human can bring against it. And it will because I have built it well.'' The Bishop paused a moment. "Why are you here?''

Peter stared up at the Bishop's head and huge eyes staring down at him, the claws. "To get funding for the HRP. That's all—I swear!''

"No. That's not what I meant.'' The Bishop resumed pacing. "You were born in Batoche, Canada. You grew up there. Your family is Metis—and stayed there even after the Metis Rebellion of 1885. You stayed there even when Dumont fled and Riel was hung by the army. Your family wouldn't leave even then, and they've been there over a hundred years and you, Peter St. Croix, have come to Boston, settled here ten years ago. Peter St. Croix, I must know: *why are you here?*''

Peter replied without thinking, without any preparation at all: "Because I killed my sister.''

"Ah!'' the Bishop stopped, sat at his desk, and watched him. It was as if the Bishop had decided he had nowhere else to go in this life, nothing more important to do than listen to Peter St. Croix. "Your sister's alive. I don't understand.''

"I—'' He stopped. It seemed very important

to say this right. "My sister and I were very different. I was one of those angry young men and my sister—Marie—was one of those cheerful people? The kind that hum under their breath when they don't know they're doing it and whistle in supermarkets. They called us the light and the dark, the *blanc et noir*."

Peter leaned back against the plywood wall: the smell of paint, wet wood, and smoke swirled around him and mingled with the remembered fumes from the tractor and the smell of freshly turned earth.

"She was on the planter and I was driving the tractor. The sun was high and the air was bright blue and the grass was green—one of those early summer days up in the north country. You could see the river from the tractor. And I looked away, looked over at—towards the river. It doesn't matter at what. And the tractor lurched and Marie fell under the planter. She's paralyzed, her body and—well, everything's scarred. One arm was torn off at the elbow—they can't sew it back on when it's torn that bad. And the other is almost ruined." He held up his hands helplessly. "I couldn't stay after that. Everybody thought it was an accident, could happen to anybody, *not your fault*. I knew better." He stopped and searched for the words. "I was there the moment she awoke and I looked at her. And I knew. Whatever it was that made her the way she was I'd broken. It seemed I'd broken some kind of promise, the reason we had stayed there for so long. This was the contract: you live correctly.

You live right. And in return, you will be allowed to stay.''

"A contract with the army that killed Riel? To stay there?''

"No!'' Peter shook his head violently. "Something else. God, maybe.'' He laughed at himself. "The land. Riel. Dumont. Hell, I don't know.'' He stopped and looked up into the insectoid eyes. "Christ! What the hell am I saying? Jesus—''

"No,'' said the Bishop in his dry sticks voice. Peter stopped speaking, feeling strange but somehow completely embarrassed.

"I killed,'' the Bishop said slowly. "I killed my brother—in your language. And ate him. But to me, he was not my brother because he did not pass the test. He could not be a person; he did not have the capacity. So we, the family, in solemn ceremony, killed him mercifully and without pain, and ate him. We preserved what he might have been by doing that.'' The Bishop paused a moment. "Do you understand that?''

Peter stared into those eyes and considered it, imagined the Bishop doing that—he could see it, the group carefully dismembering a properly prepared body. He felt interested in a kind of detached way. It no more concerned him than the flight of insects or the mating dance of a spider. It was *other*.

And in realizing that, he knew that the Bishop looked at *him* in exactly the same manner; both of them knew the other was different but connected. Looking at himself this way, outside of people, made him feel free. It was enough to judge himself. Nobody else was necessary.

"Yes," said Peter at last.

"I spent an hour on the net saying that and no one understood. I've been getting fifty calls and a pound of mail an hour since."

Peter shrugged. "I wouldn't worry about it."

"I must. It is not enough merely to rule. There must be understanding or I will make great and bloody mistakes."

"Rule? What— Why are you *here*?"

"Not once has that question been asked of me." The Bishop brought his claws together and finger danced again. "When a pupa emerges from the cocoon, it is a child and it is a law that all children have a right to live until they can be tested. So must worlds be treated. So must you— all of you—be treated. It is a duty. *Rhamcha.*"

"Beg pardon?"

"*Chamcha* and *Rhamcha*. The words for duty in my language. We are different from you, obviously. And the word means a great deal more in my language than in yours." The Bishop fell silent.

"Well, sir," began Peter after a minute. "About the project—"

"Consider it taken care of. Consider it the least of your worries. Your community will not drown."

"Right." He assumed the meeting was at an end and stood.

The Bishop looked up at him. "I have a job for you, if you wish it."

Peter shook his head. "I've already got a job, sir. I'm a fisherman."

The Bishop nodded and Peter suddenly realized he must have *learned* the gesture, all gestures.

"There is no conflict." The Bishop pointed back to the chair and Peter slowly sat down.

"My assignment here is a conservatorship," the Bishop continued. "And my faith teaches that each assignment rests on three legs: the control of the Loophole, the understanding of institutions, and the relationship between the Bishop and the species. I would like to know you well."

Peter didn't say anything for a long while.

"I will pay you, of course," added the Bishop.

"You'll pay me? To be what—your friend?"

The Bishop nodded. "Yes. I have need of such a friend. I need a man who will speak with me about himself. Who has expectations of me that a human would have of another human. Who will be honest with me and share his opinions. Who I can ask questions and expect complete answers. Would that be a definition of a friend?"

"We usually like each other, too."

"That would be desirable, but not necessary." The Bishop cocked his head to one side. "What do you think?"

At first, he rejected the idea out of hand. Friends? With something that looked like a praying mantis stuck on a pill bug? Then, he remembered how easy it was to talk about Marie to the Bishop and he realized that he'd made his decision long before this.

Peter stood. "My friendship is not for sale. But I will come see you and talk to you and all that." He turned to go.

"Why?"

"Because I trust you, Bishop 24." He shook his head as he walked to the door. "Damned if I know why. For no more reason than that."

2019 10:22

From the kitchen, he could see the Hog Island docks. Right now there was enormous activity going; a truck was being carefully driven onto one of Lat Do's amphibious boats. Peter couldn't hear from inside, but he could imagine the shouts, the instructions in several languages, the rich profanity. He smiled into his coffee.

Bethel had left the room to get Sara and Roni up. They were enjoying sleeping late these days. During the school year, they were allowed to sleep until they had to go to school. Then, he loaded the boat by himself with hired help. Now, it was summer and in a week or so, when he left again for the banks, they'd help him and be getting up early as hell. Between now and then, they were allowed to sleep late. Roni might come with him this year. Sara had been helping him the last three years and she hated it. Maybe Roni wouldn't feel the same.

He turned back to the kitchen and Gabriel was sitting at the table staring mournfully at Bethel's

coffee cup. "One of the many things I miss."
He sighed.

Peter ignored him and started gathering together materials for the kids' breakfast.

"Peter," said Gabriel solemnly. "On this day with so much happening, can't you talk with an old friend?"

"You're no friend of mine."

"You didn't think so, once."

Peter looked at him. "I learned. Marie taught me that."

Gabriel flinched as if he'd been hit. "She looks well enough now."

"That's due to Lat Do. Not you."

"Nor you," said Gabriel mildly.

Outside he heard the deep-throated rumble of a truck rolling up the road to the house. Peter left Gabriel and stepped outside.

Several men jumped off the truck, shouting at each other in a language Peter didn't recognize. One man, tall and dark, came over to Peter. "Where do you want?" he said in heavily accented English. European—Czech, Peter decided. He'd heard Lat Do had made some deal in Prague.

"What is it?" he asked. Lat Do had sent something over again. Since Marie had moved to Hog Island, he'd taken to sending gifts over every now and then. Peter had protested it wasn't necessary, or even desirable, that he do this. Their friendship didn't need it. Lat Do continued to agree and promise not to send anything else.

A promise which he would keep faithfully for about a week.

The Czech answered something unintelligible and Peter shook his head. Frustrated, the Czech shouted something in Burmese and the tarp on the back of the truck was removed.

It was a rocket launcher.

"My God," breathed Peter as he walked up to the truck.

"Fire-uh-fly," said the Czech. "Very powerful. Simple. A child could use."

"I can't take this!" Peter cried. "Wait. You wait right here. Don't do anything—anything at all! I'll be right back."

He ran back in the house and dialed Lat Do's private number. His smiling face, complete with cigarette, appeared before Peter. "Do you like it? Isn't it pretty?"

"What the hell are you giving me this for?"

Lat Do laughed. "Can't have my brother-in-law unsafe. The MDC could bomb us any day."

"You leave that here and they'll level this place!"

"No problem." Lat Do waved that away, pulled on his cigarette. "It'll be camouflaged. No one will notice—at least no one in an MDC plane. They don't have the right military hardware."

"You get that thing out of here!"

Lat Do shook his head. "No can do, fellow. I need insurance."

"I can't even shoot the damned thing!"

"Sure you can. Push three buttons to get it

ready. You can figure it out. It's got a trigger—point the sights at a plane and pull it. It's smart enough to do the rest. It's the best—Japan designed, India made." Lat Do looked off the screen. "Got to go. See you soon, maybe." He laughed and blanked the screen.

Outside, he heard the truck starting. Peter ran to the door and saw the truck drive away back down to the docks. The back of the truck was empty.

Below his kitchen window, carefully camouflaged, the launcher had been assembled, aimed to the south. Exactly from where an MDC might fly. The absurdity of it got to him.

"Damn you, Lat Do." Peter sat down on the grass and started laughing. "Damn you to hell."

2015

It was spring. The whaler was moored at the jetty next to the seawall and Peter was loading in the new fish-finder electronics. Gabriel was standing on the wall, thinking out loud over the sorry state of the soil down here, and how much better it was in Batoche. On the long row of poplars he'd planted on his homestead, the sound the leaves made when the wind blew down the river valley, how the army had burned the houses when they came—

"Hello!"

Peter looked up and saw an Oriental man looking down at him from the wall. The man was impeccably dressed in a gray suit. He pulled a cigarette case from inside his jacket, carefully chose a cigarette from inside it and lit it, replaced the case. There was an overpowering grace to the motions.

"How do you do?" the man said in a vaguely English accent.

Peter straightened and nodded. "Fine. What can I do for you?"

"My name is Lat Do," he announced in a manner that suggested it was a fine and a good name. "I'm considering living around here. I am looking around."

Peter continued loading the whaler. Lat Do smoked on the wall and watched the sea.

"Where are you from?" Peter asked as he worked.

"Hong Kong." Lat Do exhaled a rich, exotic smoke. "I was one of the Chairman's refugees in 1997. I've been around. I see you've lost the houses down the hill."

"Yeah. Lost the last of them out to sea two winters back. Where are you guys thinking of buying?"

"Not down there; that's for sure." Lat Do chuckled. "I do not yet know. How many people live here?"

"Maybe twenty families. Eight, actually on this side of the hill. More, scattered around."

"Twenty families," Lat Do said in an abstracted voice. "About a hundred or so people?"

"Something like that." Peter finished loading up the boat and came up to the sea wall and sat down. Lat Do continued to pace, watching everything—the sky, the water, the hill, the spit—like a very intent bird.

"What kind of business are you in? This is a hell of a place to live if it doesn't suit you." Peter dried his hands. It seemed no matter what you did with a boat you always got your hands wet and he didn't like the feel of the Boston harbor water.

Lat Do grinned at him. "Import and export, Mister St. Croix. There's a whole new world opening up, now that we have visitors."

"I didn't tell you my name."

"But I told you mine. Isn't it only right that I should know yours? I know everybody's name on this island, Mr. St. Croix. I am a good businessman and a good businessman knows his neighbors."

"You didn't need to be asking me, I suppose."

"Always have to be polite and ask." He pointed out across the water. "Is that your boat out there?"

Gabriel stood next to Lat Do and peered closely in his eyes. "Make no mistake," Gabriel said to Peter softly. "He knows whose boat that is."

Peter ignored him and spoke directly to Lat Do. "Yes. That's the *Hercules*. Paid for last year. We had a hell of a party for that, I can tell you."

"I can imagine." Lat Do squatted down next to Peter. "My people have been on boats forever. Up and down the Yellow River for generations, then to Hong Kong a hundred years ago, and now here. I know boats. That looks like one that's well taken care of.''

''Thanks.''

''I'm looking to hire a few boats.''

Gabriel leaned next to him. ''Don't trust him. He's a smuggler. And British, no matter what color his skin.''

''I don't think so, Mr. Lat Do—''

''Just Lat Do. No 'Mister'. May I call you Peter?''

''I'm a fisherman. I couldn't tell you when I'd have the boat in port.''

''Ah, I see.'' Lat Do looked out to sea, finished his cigarette, and tossed it out to sea. ''It's a whole new world out there, Mister St. Croix. There'll be plenty of work for everybody, if you should change your mind. We shall be good neighbors, I think.'' He bowed slightly to Peter. ''Have a pleasant day.''

With that, Lat Do walked further on down the wall, around the bend in the island, out of sight.

''There goes,'' mused Gabriel quietly, ''one dangerous man.''

2019 11:04

Peter walked up the stairs of the old watchtower. By the time he reached the top, he was breathing heavily. Two hundred steps, and he remembered each one. At the top, he could see Boston in the distance, and in the harbor, the half completed IPOB tower.

He'd come up here to see if he could tell what the MDC was doing, from the writing of jets in the sky, the signature of boats in the harbor. He scanned the shoreline with binoculars. Nothing. If the MDC decided to bomb Hull, the planes would fly down from the MDC wing in Worcester. If they came by boat, it would be from Hingham, just a few miles away. *One if by air, two if by sea*. There was no middle ground: Hull was a pair of islands, now. *One if by air, two if by sea*. But who would he tell?

He walked slowly down to the ground and then back to the house, got his bicycle, and rode down the hill to the school. People were waiting for him there in the lunchroom.

There weren't many: Friedrich Wilton and his family, Frank Cobb and his wife—their kids had already moved to the mainland. Coretta LaRue and her oldest son. Coretta's husband, Ray, had disappeared off the side of the *Hercules* when Peter and Ray had been fishing off the bank four years ago. They'd never found the body. Coretta never seemed to blame Peter, but Peter had worked with strangers after that, hired men out of Boston Seaman's Hall and out of New Bedford. He didn't want to ever lose another friend.

They quieted when he entered and leaned his bicycle against the wall. Bethel was there with Roni and Sara. That irritated him, but he didn't say anything. He thought she'd taken the kids to the *Hercules*.

He sat next to her.

"We were just waiting for you, Peter," said Frank.

"Right." He stood up. "Okay. Here's what you know: the MDC has committed to evicting Lat Do from Hog Island. They might deport him—to where is a good question, but it doesn't concern us. Lat Do says he isn't going. And he'll fight. Nobody wants that, especially us. IPOB is backing the MDC on this and nobody wants to bring in the state. So it's all local. That's what we knew."

Peter stopped and waited for any questions. None came. "Okay. They won't bomb unless we leave. And we won't leave because if we do, there's not going to be much left of our homes. I've been talking and talking to everybody that'll listen to me. Nothing much has changed. So what do you want me to do?"

Several people spoke up at once, stopped because of the resulting babble, and sorted themselves out.

Winston Boone, the old man who lived in the cradle of the sea wall on the north side, stood up. "I got nowhere else to go. If God comes for me, I'll go with Him, but I'll go with no man."

"That's all right for you, Winston," cried Coretta. "And it's okay by me. But I got three sons and a daughter here. Has Commissioner James offered any relocation plans?"

Peter spread his hands. "Nothing new: they'll move us into Hingham or Plymouth. It's either bomb us or do nothing. They say Lat Do is in too good a position to do anything different. I'll tell you: I don't want to go. My wife's family has had that house since nineteen twenty. We moved in there in twenty oh-two, right after her parents passed away. It's our home."

Friedrich stood up. "If they will give us guns, we will take care of Lat Do ourselves. Have them do that for us."

Peter remembered the launcher in his front yard. "We can't do that."

"You say that because Lat Do is your brother-in-law."

"You're right." Peter nodded. "And when the big storm knocked a hole in your foundation and broke the power lines it was Lat Do who sent in his men to repair your house in the middle of the night. Two men nearly died so that you and your family could stay warm. And when the water line broke and the Water Commission said they weren't going to fix it—we would have to move. It was Lat Do who had it repaired and paid for it." Peter looked around them. "Lat Do's a smuggler—we all know it. And the MDC has good reasons to shut him down. But he's been a good neighbor to us."

"Sure," said Coretta. "As long as we're here, he's safe."

"I suppose," Peter conceded. "But some kind of war with the city of Boston isn't going to help anybody. Let's put it to a vote. Who's going to stay?"

Louis Riel strode into the room, looked around at them. "Are you strong enough? Are your pure enough? Are you *men*? Are you going to let them carry off the very land you have fought for? That you've died for? First it was Red River and Fort Garry. We fought and lost. Then, it was Batoche and they tried to take our land with a pen, and when we refused, with the sword! What manner of men would lie down before this! God has come with us into this land. He spread his cloak before us and made our lives rich. God did not bring us here to leave us to die. He will fight for us now. Rise up!'' He stared at them. ''Rise up and fight them! Make them give you what is yours!'' He stopped and the thunder of his voice echoed in the lunchroom. Peter's breath caught in his throat and tears came to his eyes. *Yes!*

Louis held up his hands. ''I have a vision. It is a vision given me by my Maker. We will fight here. We will keep this, our place. And we will be *victorious*!''

''Yes,'' whispered Peter.

''Peter?'' said Coretta.

Peter looked at her, then back at Louis. Louis was gone.

''Peter? We were going to vote.'' Coretta looked at him, surprise on her face.

Woula that I could speak with your voice, Louis.

''A vote. Who's going to stay?''

He'd hoped to carry them but he could see from the closed doors of their faces that most of them were too scared to stay. The vote went against him. Even Frank had given up. Again, he wished for Louis' power. But that was for a stronger people and a more naive time.

"I will stay," said Winston. "The rest of you can leave, but I will stay."

"Me, too," said Peter, looking at Bethel. "My family and I owe Lat Do a special debt. We're going to stay."

Bethel looked away.

2016

"Wake up!" An urgent whisper. "Wake up!"

He woke from a sound sleep, wondering what had awakened him. In the distance, he could hear something—a party, maybe—going on over at the island. That wouldn't wake him.

Gabriel was standing over him and as he watched, Gabriel faded.

A faint cry. A faint whimper. It was Roni, crying.

Bethel woke up when he left the bed. He took the pistol from the nightstand and padded quietly down the hall to Roni's room. A crying sound. A low stream of abuse—a man's voice.

He pushed the door open slowly. He could see by the moonlight a man straddling Roni, pinning her arms beneath the bedclothes. The man was completely absorbed in Roni—her eyes were terrified.

Peter crept in behind the man—could he have a knife? A gun? He swung the gun as hard as he could at the man's head. He felt the impact clear to his elbow. The man fell off the bed against the wall and was still.

"Are you all right?" Peter kept the pistol pointed at the man. "Answer me."

She gasped hard and retched across the bed.

Bethel came in the room behind him and turned on the light.

The man was a young Asian. To Peter's surprise, he was only unconscious. Peter had hit him as hard as he could; he had expected the man to be dead. The man must have moved just before Peter had hit him.

He tied the man up and stood looking at him. The man's pants were down and blood from his scalp had flowed across his chest and back. Peter looked at the scalp wound. It was ragged but already beginning to clot. The man groaned.

Peter jumped back and brought the gun up.

"Kill him," said Roni quietly.

"Huh?"

"I want him dead." Her voice was tight.

Peter looked at Bethel. Bethel looked back. Peter lowered the gun. "I don't think I can, now."

Roni looked up at him and her face made him cold. "You don't know what he said to me. You don't know what he was going to do. I know. I know because he told me every word. You don't know." Her breathing was ragged. "Kill him."

"Bethel—" Peter said. "Take care of her, will you?"

Bethel took Roni in her arms and led her out

of the room. She stopped in the doorway. "You going to do it?"

"I'll take care of it."

After they left, he squatted in front of the man and slapped his face a few times. The man opened his eyes and stared at Peter vaguely.

"Come on," said Peter. "Let's walk."

The Asian staggered down to the dock and passed out in the whaler. Peter started the engine and let it idle for a long time. Kill him? It was one of Lat Do's men—even he could tell that. Kill him? Take him out to sea and dump him in the harbor? He knew where the sharks were— there'd be nothing left in an hour.

Dawn was just wrinkling the sky.

"I'm no murderer," he muttered and swung the wheel around. He brought the boat over to Hog Island and yelled up at the guards, demanding to see Lat Do. He didn't know what they would do, just kept on yelling at them until he heard Lat Do's voice behind the spotlights saying something unintelligible.

Lat Do came out on the dock dressed in an elegant silk robe, rubbing his eyes and yawning. "Peter, my friend. What is going on?"

Peter pointed towards the boat. "He tried to rape my daughter."

"My God! Sara?"

"Roni. He pinned her down—I stopped him before he'd actually done anything."

"How is she?"

"Bethel is taking care of her. I got to get back."

"Just a moment." Lat Do turned to the guards and shouted something in a different language—a patois of Japanese and Czech and other languages. Two guards came out of the lights and took the unconscious man away.

"What's going to happen to him?"

Lat Do looked up at Peter and his eyes were flat and dark. "I can assure you this will never happen again."

A short buttery man came running out from the gates. "You called me?"

"Doctor Wentworth, this is Peter St. Croix. His daughter was attacked by one of my men. Go with him and see to her."

The doctor got into the boat.

"Go, now, Peter. Apologize for me. I will be over later to apologize for myself, when she has had a chance to rest."

"Roni wants to kill him. I'd rather my daughter didn't feel that sort of thing."

Lat Do's face hardened. "I don't blame you. I don't blame her. It is a hard world we live in, made harder if we can't protect our family. I assure you: this will never happen again."

He ferried the doctor back over to his house. Inside, the doctor was all concern and medical competence. This was no quack. He spoke with Roni for a long time. Peter could hear the two of them through the door, short, direct, reassuring sentences. Afterwards, Roni seemed more comfortable. The doctor stayed until morning. Bethel and Peter watched over her while she slept.

Once, outside in the dawning sky, Peter spoke to the air: "Thank you, Gabriel. Thank you for my daughter."

In the afternoon, she awoke and Lat Do came by. He came in and gave solemnly to Roni the promise he'd given to Peter during the night: she no longer had anything to fear. She seemed to believe him.

Later, Peter walked with Lat Do down to the docks. "What happened to him? The man last night."

"You don't want to know."

"I brought him to you. I have a part in it."

Lat Do stopped and looked out to sea. "It's taken care of."

"Who was he?"

"My brother."

"Christ!" Peter swung away from him and back again. "Did you kill him?"

"Yes."

"Christ! To kill your own brother!"

Lat Do gave him a little smile. "Who should I chose? My brother who would be a rapist or my friend who has brought me into his house? My brother who would bring down everything to satisfy his animal cravings or my friend who would lay down his life for his daughter? Who is more worthy?"

"He's your brother."

"I did my duty by him," snarled Lat Do. "He was rotting in China and I brought him here." Lat Do composed himself. "A small choice, really. I owe you and your neighbors in many ways far more than I ever owed him.''

All Peter could see was Marie. ''But your own brother—''

''It's done!'' Lat Do stepped into his boat. ''Would you have Roni stay afraid, knowing I wouldn't do what must be done to protect her? Knowing you could not? There is a saying in your country: a man must shoot his own dog. I saw my duty and I did it.'' He spoke to the man at the wheel, and the boat pulled away from the dock. ''A man can ask no more of himself.''

2019 13:40

After the vote, he rode his bike around the island, under the oak and maples and pine. There were a number of old houses, empty for years and gradually falling in on themselves. Living on the island was not easy.

He had a hope of staying, but not much of one. He had a plan he was following, but he had little hope of success. The hopelessness in him had become a sort of bleak melancholy. Meandering back to the house, he saw that the *Hercules* was still out at the mooring. Bethel had to be inside.

Peter stopped at the missile launcher and looked through the sights. It seemed a dead piece of metal. There were a series of colored lights over a set of three covered toggle switches labeled: READY, SET, and GO. He suspected Lat Do had relabeled them. He fingered them but did not lift the covers. After a few minutes, he returned to the house.

Bethel was waiting for him in the kitchen.

"What the *hell* is that thing in the front yard?" Bethel spat. "Do we store arms for terrorists now? Get that damned thing out of here!"

"It was a present from Lat Do."

"I don't care if it's a present from King Charles. Get it out of here."

"I can't send it back to Lat Do just yet." Peter sat down and stared blankly at the phone.

"Why not? Do we have to wait for it to get *bombed* out of the front lawn?"

"No. I'm waiting for something. I'm sure Lat Do's heart is in the right place. He sent it over for protection."

"Protection!" Bethel leaned against the sink. "Look. I like the little guy. I always have from the first time he came over for dinner. I like what he did for Marie. I like the way he's been a good neighbor. I'm grateful he took care of that— animal that attacked Roni."

"It was his brother." Peter closed his eyes tiredly.

"So what?" said Bethel belligerently. "That's not my fault. But what he's doing is illegal! You deal in illegalities and you deal with illegal people. You deal with illegal people and you are going to get hurt. Do you think nobody's going to notice that we have a missile launcher in our *front yard*?"

"It's camouflaged."

"Camouflaged!"

"I can't move it today!" he shouted. "I can't make any waves with him. It'll wreck everything." He quieted down. "Even you being here can wreck everything."

She didn't speak immediately. "What are you doing?"

"I can't tell you."

"You *will* tell me. I'm not leaving until you do."

They fought with their eyes for a long minute.

"Okay," he said. "The Bishop and I have been talking about the Bishop buying Lat Do out. If the Bishop will do it, it legitimizes Lat Do's operation. Nobody's going to mess with the Bishop—too much is riding on what he does. Lat Do's operation is fairly clean—he's not dealing with drugs or people or whatever. He deals with uncleared technology. The Bishop says we need something to compete with the Boston trading groups. I don't know why. He says it's important to start competition early. So he was already thinking of setting up a company and this looked promising. But it's really delicate. I've been talking to the Bishop and Marie's been talking to Lat Do. Both of them are touchy."

"What's this got to do with the launcher?"

"Lat Do sent that over this morning. All day I've been waiting for a call from the Bishop to set up a meeting. He's going to come *here*. Then he, Marie, Lat Do, and I will try to make a deal. If we can do that, then Commissioner James is tied up—attacking Lat Do would be the same as attacking Bishop 24. IPOB would close him down in a minute. I don't want to jiggle Lat Do when I'm this close. It's not much of a hope, but it's something.''

"Hm.'' She turned to look at the missile launcher.

"You've got to leave, too,'' Peter said.

"Why?''

"Why?'' he exploded. "Because if things fall apart this place is going to get flattened, that's why! Because I want you all to live. Because one of us *has* to live to take care of the kids.''

Bethel turned back to him. "Screw this place.''

"Beth—''

"Screw the Bishop, Lat Do, and Marie! Let's leave now. Let them flatten Hull. Let them flatten Hog Island. We can live on the boat—we've done it before. Come on, Peter! This isn't some game: this is life and death.''

She stretched her hand out to Peter and he reached for it, touched it briefly, and let it fall.

"No,'' he said.

"For God's sake, this is just a goddamned four bedroom colonial with a two-acre lot and a view of the ocean. That's all it is.''

Peter shook his head and looked around the kitchen. "No. It's my home. It's the only home I've got. I can't let them destroy it.''

Peter's mother died the year Roni was born. Peter's father held on several more years, taking care of Marie and renting the farm until he just grew too tired. One August, Marie found him, cold and shrunken, sitting in the living room before the video.

Peter flew to Winnipeg and took the train to Batoche, watching the fields of ripened corn and wheat mowed down by an endless steam of harvesters. It seemed distant now, unreal; it did not touch him. He expected Gabriel or Louis to follow him—hoped it, actually. Hoped they would stay there in Batoche and leave him. They did not appear at all.

He rented a small truck and drove it out to the farm. Marie met him in the front yard, her mechanized wheelchair navigating the lawn easily.

"Hey, sailor!" she said with a crooked grin.

For a moment, he was almost fooled. He searched her eyes and looked for that light he remembered. It was not there. He hugged her to him, happy to see her, thinking maybe that light he'd seen had never really been there, had only been a product of his youth.

Over the next few days, they sold the farm and either sold or gave away the equipment in bits and pieces until there was only a small pile left. Small enough to fit on the truck.

Marie watched him load the last of it. "You know," she said, "I feel as if I am at the beginning of a great adventure." She waved the stump of her right arm and the ruined left. "Let's get this show on the road."

It was a long drive to Boston—difficult in some ways for there were a number of problems due to Marie's bent and broken body. It was good in others. Marie spent hours staring out the window as they drove through Montana, Minnesota, gasped at the lights of Chicago.

"You never told me anything about any of this," she complained. "You never described this in your letters. When you called it was just, 'dropped down to New Bedford to hire this guy or that guy.' Never anything about the lights. Never anything about the hills or the roads. I know. You wanted to surprise me."

There was nothing else he could have said: "Of course."

And then they both laughed.

Hull was something else entirely. She didn't like it at all: "There's all of Boston over there and we never even go there!" or "This place is even smaller than Batoche. At least at home, I could drive the chair out away from the house a little ways." A month after he returned, Marie fell silent and Peter didn't know what to do.

Lat Do invited himself over for dinner one night, bringing steak from Colorado. A gift, he said, from a satisfied client.

He showed up at their door dressed impeccably, as always. He brought flowers for Marie.

She held them in her lap and smiled shyly at him—which surprised Peter. He'd never known Marie to be shy about anything.

Lat Do bowed and kept them entertained with a steady stream of jokes and stories from Hong Kong.

At the end of the night, he kissed Marie's only hand and left.

Peter had been watching her and looked away then. He had been watching her face all evening, afraid for her, happy for her. He recognized the light in her face.

2019 15:09

Peter stared at the phone for an hour and it didn't ring. He tried not staring at it. Again nothing. He worked in the garden, moved around the house. He walked the two hundred steps to the watchtower again and tried to read the day in sign: the shapes of clouds, the pattern of sun on water. Nature told him little, but he could see boats leaving Hull, boats he recognized. Coretta's lobster boat was chugging mightily towards Boston, followed closely by various other boats. All of them neighbors. He couldn't see Winston Boone's boat, but Winston had said he would stay. There were a few other boats he missed. Peter figured they had already left or would be leaving shortly.

Bethel called up to him and he ran down, taking the steps four at a time. He was out of breath when he reached the kitchen.

"Peter," said the Bishop, "were you working hard in your garden? You're sweaty."

"Right. Yeah."

"I have called to tell you I will be coming to Hull about four-thirty. This is a secret meeting—can you persuade the other party to attend?"

"Can I?" Peter grinned. "If I have to frog march him."

"Beg pardon?"

"Never mind. How about the school? You can bring a boat right to the school dock and no one will be able to see you. Lat Do can be discrete as well. Come to the lunchroom."

"Very good. I will see you then." The Bishop's face disappeared.

"Hot damn!" Peter laughed as he dialed Marie. After a moment, her face appeared. As always, he was amazed at the difference: the scars were gone. Her ruined arm was fully functional and there was a disconcertingly alive prosthetic on the other. She was still confined to a wheelchair, but she was able to walk on occasion. Lat Do had used every piece of alien technology he could find to help Marie. It was as if he had brought the dead to life.

"Hey, sailor," she said.

"We got a live one. The Bishop. Now the ball's in your court."

Her face grew serious. "When and where?"

"Four-thirty. In the lunchroom of the school. Can you do it?"

Marie nodded. "Absolutely." And disappeared.

"This thing's going to work, then?" Bethel asked from behind him.

He turned to her. "We've really got a chance. But you have to leave. They'll be here in an hour."

Bethel nodded unhappily. "I have some things I want to get out to the *Hercules*. Then I'll take the girls. I don't like it."

Peter hugged her. "I know. Hopefully, it'll just be a shopping trip." He ran downstairs and gathered up his notes of the last few weeks. Outside, he started to ride to the school when he saw Louis examining the missile launcher.

"Get away from there!" he cried, a cold bolt of fear running from spine to brain and back again. Could he trigger the missiles? He'd never seen Louis touch anything, ever. Peter ran to the launcher.

"What are you doing?" he said furiously.

Louis turned to him calmly. "Inspecting the arms."

"You leave that alone. We're going to win this and I don't want you screwing it up."

"As you wish, Peter," said Louis. "Take the gun."

"Gun?"

"There's a pistol in your bedroom. Take it."

"I won't need it."

"Take it anyway."

Peter bit his lip, thinking. He ran back inside and took the pistol and stuffed it in his jacket. Outside again, he called to Louis. "Does that make you happy?"

"Very much so. I'll be waiting here for you when you return."

"We're not going to have to fight this time."

"I hope not," said Louis quietly. "I always hope not."

2019 16:04

The lunchroom was deserted. Peter spent the hour reviewing his notes hastily. Reading the same sections over and over, trying to calm down. There was a hollowness to the school—to the whole island, now. Peter didn't know if anybody was left on the island, but he doubted it. The island felt like an empty room.

The Bishop entered from the back of the lunchroom. Peter looked up and watched him approach. The Bishop moved stately, but with the air of restrained power. Always, there was that jerkiness to his movements, as if he were holding himself back.

"Peter, my friend," he said and held out his claw.

Peter touched the claw lightly. "Sir. Lat Do and my sister will be here shortly."

"Good." The Bishop leaned back against the base of his body the way a man leans back in a rocking chair. "I brought only a small launch. We must be discrete."

"Yes, sir."

"Peter!" cried Lat Do as he entered with Marie. They walked past the Formica lunch tables towards them. Marie was walking with him.

"Check this out," said Lat Do with a wide grin. "My wife's got legs!"

Marie smiled. "I've been practicing."

"That's great." Peter looked at them, then at the Bishop. He cleared his throat. "May I introduce you to Bishop 24."

Lat Do looked up at the Bishop, held out his hand, and smiled. "Good day to you, sir. I understand we have something to discuss."

The Bishop touched his hand with his claw and nodded. "I hope so."

With that, sitting across the lunch tables from one another, they got down to business.

"Let me open," said the Bishop. "I have discovered something about Commissioner James' approach to your operation. He plans to use new armaments purchased from various extraterrestrial vendors against your operation. It is to be all-out war. 'Scorched earth' is, I believe, the correct term."

"He will not find us unprepared." Lat Do chuckled. "We are not naive."

"True. But you don't have access to his materials."

"You'd be surprised to what I have access."

"Mister Lat Do—"

"Just Lat Do, please."

"Lat Do," continued the Bishop. "I know exactly to what you have access. I know because I have allowed it. Commissioner James has better and more powerful weapons."

Marie stared at the Bishop for a long moment.

"I'll be damned," she said softly. "You planned this."

Lat Do looked at her, then at the Bishop. "You're right."

Peter looked from one to the other. "What's going on?"

"Peter, the son of a bitch *planned* this. It all makes sense now!"

Peter tried to see all of them at once: Marie, the Bishop, Lat Do. "I don't understand."

Lat Do didn't take his eyes off the Bishop. "The leaks of technology. The connections I made. Specific groups of inventions—he planned it. He leaked it all. He said Boston needed the competition—remember? He set us up to be that competition. I always figured it was the incompetent bureaucrats, bribable officials that made it easy. I always figured it was me buying protection. But no." He breathed admiringly. "It was *him*. Leading me here. And now, now that he needs us to come out in the open, he's brought the pressure to bear on us. He created this whole situation."

"Commissioner James—" began Peter.

"Peter, you're a nice guy and you have a hell of a sister. But you're not too sophisticated. *Commissioner James is his man!*"

Peter shook his head and asked the Bishop: "Is this true?"

"Not entirely." The Bishop did not move. "Security of incoming goods can never be perfect and I knew there would be leaks. I just made sure the leaks were where and what I wanted.

Boston had a trading establishment in place and it needed competition, or ideas, goods, and individuals would never get established. They would upset too many conventions. It is important that the inflow is controlled, but not by humans, by me. It is *Rhamcha*."

The Bishop held his claws together. "However, I 'own' nobody. I merely have influence. People do things on their own—if they didn't there would be no need of me here." He pointed at Lat Do. "I did not choose Lat Do. I just made sure someone like Lat Do could thrive. He built his operation, not me. And now, I would like him to work as a competitor in the open. As a sort of partner."

Peter frowned. "I don't like this."

Lat Do slapped him on the back. "Peter, you're outclassed. I'm outclassed. That's no sin. Now we'll have to make the best of it. Your Grace, your Excellency, your Holiness, I accept your offer of purchase. What else can I do?"

The Bishop nodded. "Very little."

There was a dull sound of distant thunder.

Each of them fell silent. Thunder came again and a gentle rocking of the building. Plaster fell from the ceiling.

Lat Do turned easily towards the Bishop but now the laughter was gone. It was the easy movement of a snake.

"Commissioner James has come to join us, I see."

"I mentioned people do things on their own." The Bishop straightened up and seemed to loosen up his arms. "They even make mistakes. Commissioner James is not here at my request. This is not my doing."

Lat Do looked at Marie. "You did say, 'scorched earth.' You would know." He pulled out a gun and pointed it at the Bishop. "My wife's not going to die because of your mistake. You came here in a boat. You're going to take us away in it."

"For Christ's sake!" cried Peter. "He's the Bishop—the whole damned planet goes down the tube if you kill him."

"He's right," said the Bishop conversationally. "The Sh'k or the Targives will gut this planet down to bedrock without me here. My order keeps the peace."

"Your order isn't worth my spit!" cried Lat Do. "My wife and I are going to leave with you."

The Bishop did not move. "There is only room enough for me."

"Fine. Give me the keys."

The Bishop produced a box-shaped object. "I am too important to leave to chance." He threw the box in a blinding move and struck Lat Do in the throat. The gun fired twice, wildly. Lat Do collapsed on himself, choking and thrashing. Peter and Marie ran to his side. His throat was crushed. Marie tried to open it but Lat Do went into convulsions and snapped at her fingers, fell still.

Marie stared at Lat Do's body. She took the gun from Lat Do's hand and looked at it, looked at Peter and back to Lat Do. She picked up the box and tossed it to the Bishop. "Take it and be damned."

She aimed the gun slowly at the Bishop. The Bishop dropped his arms and stared back at her.

"Marie," whispered Peter. "Don't. Not him."

"*You* toady up to him! I won't. I don't care who he is."

"Marie, he's too important!"

"No one but Lat Do was ever that important to me."

Peter pulled out his own gun. Marie looked at him, then back at the Bishop.

"*Marie!*"

She started to squeeze the trigger and Peter shot her.

Marie crumpled on top of Lat Do. Peter cried out and pulled her to him, tilted up her face. She looked up at him and there, before his eyes, he saw the light die.

Distant thunder. A light fixture fell crashing to the floor. The room shook slowly, patiently. Peter stood up swaying with the room. He turned to the Bishop. "Why didn't you kill her? You killed Lat Do."

"I couldn't kill my friend's sister."

Peter laughed hollowly. "Of course not. Only I could do that." Tears fell down his cheeks. "Go on. Get the hell out of here. I hate you but you're too damned important to die."

The Bishop moved slowly away.

"Go on. *Get out of here!*"

The Bishop was gone.

After a moment, Peter, too, was gone, and there was only the sound of breaking glass and cracking buildings. People were only a memory.

2019 16:30

"Get in the boat," Bethel said to Roni and Sara. "Come on. We haven't been to Boston for a long time."

She stopped. On the other side of the boat, standing on the water, was Marie, looking back at her.

"Marie?" said Bethel softly. But it wasn't Marie. This was a girl, barely seventeen. This was Marie whole and unbroken, standing on the water barefoot and looking back at her.

Bethel heard the jets coming in from the south. "Oh, Christ. Oh, Christ. Get to the boat! Get to the boat!" Bethel jumped into the boat after them and started the engine. Marie stood there, looking at her.

Peter!

"Go on," Bethel said as she scrambled back onto the dock. "Go on to the *Hercules*. We'll meet you there!' She ran up the stairs back towards the house without looking back.

Peter didn't remember walking back to the house. Suddenly, he was there in the front yard. Gabriel and Louis stood next to him as he watched the MDC planes dive towards Hog Island. The island sprouted guns and missile launchers and on the other side of the east hill, the emplacements Lat Do had installed were firing at the planes as they passed. Winston Boone sat next to the launcher, calmly watching the planes fly over.

"The army has attacked," shouted Gabriel.

"God is with us!" cried Louis.

Bethel grabbed him from behind. "For God's sake, Peter. Let's get out of here."

Peter stared deep into her eyes. He had never loved her more than right at that moment. He turned away from her and sat at the missile launcher, stared at the switches. He flicked the switch marked READY.

"Peter," said Louis. "Do what must be done."

"Peter!" cried Bethel.

"Marie is dead."

The light flickered on and he pushed down the SET switch.

"But we aren't," cried Bethel.

"I may as well be. Go on," Peter looked at her. "I'm staying. This is all there is."

Bethel didn't say anything for a moment. "Move over, Winston. Make a place for me."

The third light flickered on and he pushed down the GO switch. He closed his eyes and listened to the jets screaming through the air, the razor blades of the missiles, the dull concussions of the explosions.

Peter opened his eyes. Death had entered his heart. There was death in his eyes, death in his hands.

He looked through the launching sight and started firing. Through it he saw them coming, riding towards him on white horses, firing their muskets, their coats bright red, their brass buttons glinting fire.

Epilog: 2019

To understand a Centaur you must understand context.

A Centaur's mind is not like that of a man's. Where a man's mind is free-flowing image—movement, sound, color—a Centaur's mind is a series of freeze-frames and sound bites. Men are continuous; Centaurs are discrete. Men are analog; Centaurs are digital. The late and lamented Thomas Ryle, who won the Nobel Prize for medicine in 2040 said that it was entirely possible that Centaurs were not intelligent or sentient at all by how we defined the term at all. Instead, their ability to determine context from imperfect data mimicked intelligence so well humans were never able to tell the difference. From this comes their nature. From this comes their abilities.

The Bishop, as he sped away from Hull in his boat, experienced a certain reluctance to leave. Duty: *Chamcha*, "to choose the moral sacrifice." *Rhamcha*, "to choose the Holy Sacrifice." Both had demanded that he leave Peter.

This reminded him of another context, that of his friendship with several of the spatiens long ago. They were labeled: dead and failed, though of late a shade had been insisting he was alive. The Bishop had dismissed it. It was a continual act of discipline to prevent the world of the apparent shade from comingling with the context of the real world.

It was twilight when he docked with Gnoza's larger boat. Gnoza said nothing but loaded the smaller launch and set a course for Rowe's Wharf. The Bishop did not attempt to converse with him. He sat on the stern viewing deck watching the smoke and flames pile high against the darkening sky.

He saw freeze-frame pictures of the missiles fired from the MDC jets, stop-motion explosion, death in still photography.

Several boats passed him, fire fighting boats and a couple of coast guard cutters hurrying towards Hull. They did not touch him. Inset against this was the memory of Lat Do, Marie, and Peter.

Gnoza brought the boat into dock and waited for the Bishop to disembark. The Bishop continued to stare southward.

After a time, he noticed a distant figure walk towards him across the water. Even in the distance, he could see Peter's shade walking towards him slowly. Shifting this way and that as the sunlight faded and the moonlight grew, as the peaceful stars came out over the water. The shade finally stopped a few meters from the boat, moving up and down slowly with the swells, fading in and out like fog or flickering shadow.

Peter had given his life for him. Out of such gifts are debts made. Out of such debts came duties: *Chamcha* and *Rhamcha*, together here. The Personal and the Holy.

"What do you want?" he asked the shade.

Peter did not speak. He just watched the Bishop.

"I will bring what remains of your family home," the Bishop said, trying to understand what Peter's shade might want.

The shade remained.

"A more benign rule over earth, perhaps. Less interference?"

No response.

The Bishop nodded—nodding seemed natural now. Many things seemed natural that once were foreign or disgusting. How one's life made one change.

He thought for a long moment and looked at the shade. "You *will* tell me what you want eventually, won't you?"

Peter was silent.

"So be it," he said, accepting it. "Come with

me, then. There is work to be done.'' The Bishop left the boat and Peter followed him. The walked back into Boston towards the Bishop's office.

Duty called.

This work came out of the project the Cambridge SF Workshop began in 1987. That project, a shared world in and around Boston, occupied the workshop for two years. The project was messy, hard, personally and professionally difficult, and roaring good fun.

People other than the workshop, though, were also necessary for "Slow Lightning" to be written. They are listed here.

Arthur Feinsod
Madeleine Robins
Kathy Romer
Valerie Smith
Sherry Stidolph
and my wife
Wendy Zimmerman

And the works of Michael Dorris and Harold Pinter.

There are, of course, always countless more people that keep you alive whether the river flows or not. Thank you all.

BESTSELLING BOOKS FROM TOR

☐ 58341-8   ANGEL FIRE by Andrew M. Greeley $4.95
☐ 58342-6   Canada $5.95

☐ 58338-8   THE FINAL PLANET by Andrew M. Greeley $4.95
☐ 58339-6   Canada $5.95

☐ 58336-1   GOD GAME by Andrew M. Greeley $4.50
☐ 58337-X   Canada $5.50

☐ 50105-5   CITADEL RUN by Paul Bishop $4.95
☐ 50106-3   Canada $5.95

☐ 58459-7   THE BAREFOOT BRIGADE by Douglas C. Jones $4.50
☐ 58460-0   Canada $5.50

☐ 58457-0   ELKHORN TAVERN by Douglas C. Jones $4.50
☐ 58458-9   Canada $5.50

☐ 58364-7   BON MARCHE by Chet Hagan $4.95
☐ 58365-5   Canada $5.95

☐ 50773-8   THE NIGHT OF FOUR HUNDRED RABBITS $4.50
☐ 50774-6   by Elizabeth Peters   Canada $5.50

☐ 55709-3   ARAMINTA STATION by Jack Vance $4.95
☐ 55710-7   Canada $5.95

☐ 52126-9   VAMPHYRI! by Brian Lumley (U.S. orders only) $4.50

☐ 52166-8   NECROSCOPE by Brian Lumley (U.S. orders only) $3.95

Buy them at your local bookstore or use this handy coupon:
Clip and mail this page with your order.

Publishers Book and Audio Mailing Service
P.O. Box 120159, Staten Island, NY 10312-0004

Please send me the book(s) I have checked above. I am enclosing $_____
(please add $1.25 for the first book, and $.25 for each additional book to
cover postage and handling. Send check or money order only—no CODs.)

Name _____

Address _____

City _____ State/Zip _____

Please allow six weeks for delivery. Prices subject to change without notice.

GRAHAM MASTERTON

Buy them at your local bookstore or use this handy coupon:
Clip and mail this page with your order.

Publishers Book and Audio Mailing Service
P.O. Box 120159, Staten Island, NY 10312-0004

Please send me the book(s) I have checked above. I am enclosing $_____
(please add $1.25 for the first book, and $.25 for each additional book to
cover postage and handling. Send check or money order only—no CODs.)

Name _____

Address _____

City _____ State/Zip _____

Please allow six weeks for delivery. Prices subject to change without notice.

THE BEST IN SCIENCE FICTION

☐	54989-9	STARFIRE by Paul Preuss	$3.95
☐	54990-2		Canada $4.95
☐	54281-9	DIVINE ENDURANCE by Gwyneth Jones	$3.95
☐	54282-7		Canada $4.95
☐	55696-8	THE LANGUAGES OF PAO by Jack Vance	$3.95
☐	55697-6		Canada $4.95
☐	54892-2	THE THIRTEENTH MAJESTRAL by Hayford Peirce	$3.95
☐	54893-0		Canada $4.95
☐	55425-6	THE CRYSTAL EMPIRE by L. Neil Smith	$4.50
☐	55426-4		Canada $5.50
☐	53133-7	THE EDGE OF TOMORROW by Isaac Asimov	$3.95
☐	53134-5		Canada $4.95
☐	55800-6	FIRECHILD by Jack Williamson	$3.95
☐	55801-4		Canada $4.95
☐	54592-3	TERRY'S UNIVERSE ed. by Beth Meacham	$3.50
☐	54593-1		Canada $4.50
☐	53355-0	ENDER'S GAME by Orson Scott Card	$3.95
☐	53356-9		Canada $4.95
☐	55413-2	HERITAGE OF FLIGHT by Susan Shwartz	$3.95
☐	55414-0		Canada $4.95

Buy them at your local bookstore or use this handy coupon:
Clip and mail this page with your order.

Publishers Book and Audio Mailing Service
P.O. Box 120159, Staten Island, NY 10312-0004

Please send me the book(s) I have checked above. I am enclosing $_____
(please add $1.25 for the first book, and $.25 for each additional book to
cover postage and handling. Send check or money order only — no CODs.)

Name _____

Address _____

City _____ State/Zip _____

Please allow six weeks for delivery. Prices subject to change without notice.

POUL ANDERSON

WINNER OF 7 HUGOS AND 3 NEBULAS

☐ 53088-8	CONFLICT	$2.95
☐ 53089-6		Canada $3.50
☐ 53083-7	DIALOGUE WITH DARKNESS	$2.95
☐ 53084-5		Canada $3.50
☐ 48517-4	EXPLORATIONS	$2.50
☐ 53050-3	GODS LAUGHED	$2.95
☐ 53051-9		Canada $3.50
☐ 53068-3	HOKA! Anderson and Gordon R. Dickson	$2.95
☐ 53069-1		Canada $3.50
☐ 53079-9	A MIDSUMMER TEMPEST	$2.95
☐ 53080-2		Canada $3.50
☐ 53054-3	NEW AMERICA	$2.95
☐ 53055-1		Canada $3.50
☐ 53081-0	PAST TIMES	$2.95
☐ 53082-9		Canada $3.50
☐ 53059-4	PSYCHOTECHNIC LEAGUE	$2.95
☐ 53060-8		Canada $3.50
☐ 53073-X	TALES OF THE FLYING MOUNTAINS	$2.95
☐ 53074-8		Canada $3.50
☐ 53076-4	TIME PATROLMAN	$2.95
☐ 53077-2		Canada $3.50
☐ 53048-9	TIME WARS created by Poul Anderson	$3.50
☐ 53049-7		Canada $4.50
☐ 48561-1	TWILIGHT WORLD	$2.75

Buy them at your local bookstore or use this handy coupon:
Clip and mail this page with your order.

Publishers Book and Audio Mailing Service
P.O. Box 120159, Staten Island, NY 10312-0004

Please send me the book(s) I have checked above. I am enclosing $_____
(please add $1.25 for the first book, and $.25 for each additional book to
cover postage and handling. Send check or money order only—no CODs.)

Name _____

Address _____

City _____ State/Zip _____

Please allow six weeks for delivery. Prices subject to change without notice.

BEN BOVA

Buy them at your local bookstore or use this handy coupon:
Clip and mail this page with your order.

Publishers Book and Audio Mailing Service
P.O. Box 120159, Staten Island, NY 10312-0004

Please send me the book(s) I have checked above. I am enclosing $_____
(please add $1.25 for the first book, and $.25 for each additional book to
cover postage and handling. Send check or money order only — no CODs.)

Name _____

Address _____

City _____ State/Zip _____

Please allow six weeks for delivery. Prices subject to change without notice.

HARRY HARRISON

Buy them at your local bookstore or use this handy coupon:
Clip and mail this page with your order.

Publishers Book and Audio Mailing Service
P.O. Box 120159, Staten Island, NY 10312-0004

Please send me the book(s) I have checked above. I am enclosing $_____
(please add $1.25 for the first book, and $.25 for each additional book to
cover postage and handling. Send check or money order only—no CODs.)

Name _____

Address _____

City _____ State/Zip _____

Please allow six weeks for delivery. Prices subject to change without notice.

KEITH LAUMER

Buy them at your local bookstore or use this handy coupon:
Clip and mail this page with your order.

Publishers Book and Audio Mailing Service
P.O. Box 120159, Staten Island, NY 10312-0004

Please send me the book(s) I have checked above. I am enclosing $_____
(please add $1.25 for the first book, and $.25 for each additional book to
cover postage and handling. Send check or money order only—no CODs.)

Name _____

Address _____

City _____ State/Zip _____

Please allow six weeks for delivery. Prices subject to change without notice.

FRED SABERHAGEN

Buy them at your local bookstore or use this handy coupon:
Clip and mail this page with your order.

Publishers Book and Audio Mailing Service
P.O. Box 120159, Staten Island, NY 10312-0004

Please send me the book(s) I have checked above. I am enclosing $_____
(please add $1.25 for the first book, and $.25 for each additional book to
cover postage and handling. Send check or money order only—no CODs.)

Name _____

Address _____

City _____ State/Zip _____

Please allow six weeks for delivery. Prices subject to change without notice.